DEAD AMERICA

by

Luke Keioskie

This one's for Kylie.

The following is a
work of fiction and
any resemblance to a
real country, living
or dead, is purely
coincidental.

Chapter 1
Farewell My
Lovely

I used to be a homicide detective and even I've never seen this before. The corpse isn't moving. Sure, the Harlem and East Rivers meet here and run fast off Carl Schurz Park, and because the dead body's half in the water, half lying on the edge of the promenade, she's tugged by the current, making her rock gently. But that's all. She isn't moving. She's not Newly Dead. She's not a necro. She's really, truly dead.

Shit. The night was looking bright until now.

I toss my cigarette butt into the river and remember the day the dead came back to life. I was twelve years old when the TV started showing scenes of dead people getting up and walking around. Just like in the movies. Only these living dead didn't try to eat our brains. They didn't rampage the streets, killing and spreading some twisted disease, infecting and destroying civilisation. These weren't monsters. They were just like us. Hell, they were us; just the dead versions come back to life. They were as surprised by it all as the rest of us were.

Not her, though.

Her name is Cheryl Hampton, though just this morning her ashen faced father, Douglas Hampton III, had

2

tearfully said she preferred to be called Cherry. There's a photo of Cherry in my jacket, where she's fresh faced, bright eyed, and living. Just another sorority girl with a NYU sweatshirt and a smile that would quicken even a dead man's heart. Her father, Douglas Hampton III, gave me the photo this morning with a solemn, "Find my girl," and a nice fat retainer for my services. I'm not made of stone so I took the money and the job. Now I have to call Mr Hampton and tell him his Cherry had been found and that she isn't undead like he'd feared or alive like he'd hoped. And I'd probably have to give the money back, too. This just gets better and better.

The crime scene's a buzz of activity and apathy, your typical late night murder scene, where the cops are either moving quick to keep back the reporters on the edge of the recently set up floodlights or they're standing around longing for another cup o' joe to keep their eyes open. They barely pay attention to me – seems my years in Homicide grant me the look of a man who belongs at the scene of a murder – so I step off the promenade to get closer to the corpse.

My camera clicks when I take a picture of her, the flash glaring accusingly. You gotta love cameras. They get smaller every year while the shit they see stays the same.

Cherry's naked except for a ragged coat. I lift the hair from her face with the end of a pen, take another picture. I wade into the water a little way, shiver at the cold, take one more. I put the camera away, shaking my head. I was too late finding you, Cherry. Too late to save you. Story of my life.

"What are you doing here, Faraday?"

There's Conroy, crime scene. A sour man, stick thin, droopy brown mouse of a moustache. I've worked with him in the past, back when I was a cop, back when I'd need his help matching a bullet to a gun or a boot print to a perp. He wasn't bad. A little twisted but not bad. One of those guys who takes their work home with them. I should know. I've seen his place. More body parts than the backroom of Madame Tussaud's. Twisted.

"Scanner told me where to find you," I say to Conroy. "I've been working a missing girl case. Looks like I found her."

Conroy smirks. Here it comes. "I heard you're not a cop anymore."

"I'm not."

Conroy shrugs. He was expecting a little more from his barb but clearly his night hasn't gone to plan either. Thankfully he doesn't press it. Good. I don't want to tell the story tonight. I want to hear his.

Conroy rubs his face wearily. "I wish *I* wasn't a cop tonight."

"Whatcha got?" It had been risky getting so close to the dead body – almost as a rule cops don't like private investigators nosing around their crime scenes, especially if the PI used to be one of them – but Conroy looks like he needs a shoulder to cry on. Or someone to bounce a question off.

"White female, late teens. A laceration on her forehead indicates she may have fallen, though I'd have to take a closer look to be sure of the cause of death. Water in her lungs, but she could have been dumped. This close to Hell Gate, she could have floated all the way from Long Island Sound so it's tough to say either way until I get inside and poke around. Mind you, at this hour she could have easily been dropped from where I'm standing."

He's right. Carl Schurz Park was popular by day, especially this summer with the high temps and humid weather, but at night, besides the occasional jogger or junkie, the place is deserted. Cherry's killer could have easily taken East River Drive, parked, walked less than five minutes and dumped her in the river. Too easy. Well, easy considering Cherry didn't relive. Nowadays it's hard to dump a body. They usually sit up during the car trip.

"Any marks on her?"

"Only this," Conroy says, lifting aside the edge of the dead girl's coat and revealing a pale ankle. Etched into her skin like a brand is:

2

It's a number two, new by the looks of the scabby tissue. Homemade, as if she did it with pins and pen ink. Hampton hadn't mentioned his little angel had ink when I'd asked him for distinguishing marks. The tattoo could be a clue to who she belongs to. From what I'd heard of Cherry, she hadn't been kidnapped as Hampton thought. She was a runaway, and runaways didn't last long on the streets of New York without someone looking after them. The tattoo could mean she has a pimp. Or *had* one before she died.

I search the dead girl's coat and it looks institutional, flimsy like a hospital gown. No wallet, no cards, nothing. But tucked in an inside pocket, wedged like a discarded credit card receipt, is a crumpled matchbook for a Greenwich Village dive called THE CLOSET SKELETON. Cute. There were a lot of places like this in Manhattan now; trendy necro bars with too-clever names. It was the in thing this season. I palm the matches. Conroy is writing something on his clipboard and doesn't notice. That's good. Palming's never been my strong point.

"How long in the water?"

There's a shine in Conroy's eyes when he says, "Looks to be five, maybe six hours dead."

Ah. I was wondering what Conroy had been itching to say.

"No one's ever gone more than an hour since..." Conroy trails off.

"I know. I'm ex-homicide, remember?"

"What...what do you think, Faraday? How come she's not kicking?"

I can't answer and Conroy licks his lips, a dry sound. I'd always wondered about Conroy, about anyone working in forensic pathology really. They seemed to have a sick fascination with the dead. Then again it doesn't take a rocket scientist to work out what the dead girl would mean to someone like Conroy. Not a lot of post mortem work is needed nowadays, since anyone who dies relives about ten minutes later knowing exactly what happened to them. Kind of defeats the purpose of boys like Conroy.

I don't know who first coined the term – there's been a lot of news, a lot of talking heads with a lot of theories. We call them the Newly Dead. Outside science, they're zombies, undead, necros, or even neccers if you're one of those black sheet wearing Life Supremacists. See, it wasn't just any old dead getting up and walking around. No stinking corpses reaching from graves. Shakespeare and Lincoln and Mick Jagger ain't running 'round. The Newly Dead are people who only just died. One expert traced the Reviving back to an exact date but no one could really agree since it happened across the world at basically the same time. I saw a chat show with Frankie Montz, the dead guy generally regarded by the media as the first American zombie.

Sorry. Dead American is the preferred term. A lot of lifism around these days. Have to watch what you say in America these days.

Frankie Montz had broken his neck after falling from a ladder while he was changing a light bulb. As his plump family wailed, he stood back up, climbed the ladder and finished the job. The story goes that when he stepped down, his wife was so shocked all she did was hand him the roast beef sandwich he'd sent her into the kitchen to fetch. Funny, isn't it? America's first necro is some rube from Wisconsin. At the end of the chat show Montz thanked God for giving him a second chance and the audience applauded.

"No second chance for Cherry," I whisper, eyes on that blonde hair trailing in the murk, still somehow bold against the brown of the Hudson. "Or applause."

"You say something, Detective?" Conroy asks.

Then, from behind us: "He ain't a detective no more."

I know the voice so I keep my eyes on Roosevelt Island and the shadow of the old lighthouse. I was wondering how long it would be before he showed up. Detective Ray Gannon. My former partner and a grade A asshole.

A rough hand turns my shoulder and I'm hit with his deadman breath. He's puffing from the walk, he never did keep in shape. For a moment I imagine him having a heart attack, right here in front of me. A comforting thought. But then he'd just get right back up anyway, reborn as an undead asshole instead of a living one. Then I'd never be rid of him.

Gannon and I go way back. Grew up in Brooklyn. Went to the same elementary, made fun of the same necro kids. Altar boys at St Dorothy's. Chester A. Arthur High. Took his sister to the prom. She was easy.

Gannon was the one who was always going to cop school. He gets off on his own authority and he respects the law. I tagged along because I had nothing better to do and his dream seemed as good as any to follow. We walked a beat in Morningside where we saw our fair share of shit. Both went plain clothes at the same time, partners in Robbery, then Vice. Homicide was my choice. It sounded easy. And it was. The majority of victims remembered who killed them, and those that didn't could usually give enough clues to go by. Until Gray Gary J, that is.

Oh, and Gannon fucked my wife, too. Did I mention that?

"Do yourself a favour, Faraday – fuck off. You're contaminatin' my crime scene." Gannon always said that, *do yourself a favour*. From the red of his eyes the favour would more likely be his than mine tonight. From the looks of Cherry, it's not hard to guess why. The first person not to relive as Newly Dead washes up on his watch. The paperwork alone would drive a lesser man to drink.

"Under some pressure, Ray?" I push. "Those reporters up there should know by now that the girl hasn't relived. Their telephotos can see it. I'd hate to be in your shoes..."

Gannon chews over what my words while he chews a toothpick. His one bad habit beside adultery used to be cigarettes. I'm guessing my ex-wife made him quit, same as she did to me with me. I started again the night she left.

I light a Death cigarette, puff. They'd made a comeback since the Reliving. Can't imagine why. Gannon's mind is working.

"How long?" he puts to Conroy, ignoring me.

"Five hours, maybe more," the CSI says.

"Shit," Gannon says.

I almost feel sorry for him. Almost. "Might be tough to get an interview out of her, Ray. Glad you're on the job and not me."

"Fuck off, Faraday. Only real cops allowed." He's already turning away from me, pulling on a latex glove and hunkering down to give Cherry a look over.

Sonofabitch. A real cop, huh? If it wasn't for him I'd still be a cop and probably still have my wife. Instead I'm a low rung private investigator and my wife's in his bed. Asshole.

I can't resist stabbing him in the back on the walk away. He makes a satisfying target. "If I see a real cop, I'll let you know."

Conroy shrugs as if to say he's sorry and trails after Gannon, who's already barking orders to get the complacent beat cops out of the way. Just like the old days, all right. Except I'm walking the other way.

There's a crowd of lights lying in wait on the edge of John Finlay Walk, reporters and TV crews. Media jackals hoping for some titbits. Behind the cameras are scatterings of rubber necking necros and living night owls, their curiosity held back by the police tape. The living rub sleep from their eyes, yawn at the late hour. The necros whisper among themselves, looking towards the blue tarp Gannon cajoles two uniforms into holding up to cut off the view of the first person in twenty years who isn't the walking dead. Guess everyone's got questions tonight.

The microphones are thrust in my face before I've cleared the police tape.

"Detective! Detective!"

"What's happened here?"

"No comment," I say through gritted teeth.

I'm almost through the press of microphones when someone asks: "Faraday! Can you confirm the corpse is more than ten hours old?"

Fuck.

There she is. Dark blue suit looking freshly starched even this late at night, hair puffed like Diane Sawyer, botox keeping her dead face youthful. Well, as youthful as a necro can look, which is a lot with all the cosmetics and embalming products on the market today. She uses them all. Alison Kastle. Kastle with a K, as she always, always points out.

I met her when she covered Midtown South. Gannon and I did a few months on the beat out of there, chasing z-boys who'd wandered too far south from Harlem, rousting formalin junkies from the park behind New York Public Library, stuff like that. Kastle had been a living woman back then. Five years later, she's a talking corpse and I'm helping her fill out a statement about the Newly Dead greaseball who slit her throat for thirty bucks in change. I've never been able to get rid of her since.

"No comment, Kastle," I say, making a growl of her name. Not being a cop anymore doesn't change the fact that old habits die hard. I don't want to be the one who tells the world Cherry Hampton's not a necro.

But Kastle isn't looking for an answer from me. She already knows the answer, even as her question ripples through the crowd.

The necros blink at one another, speechless at the implications, while the reporters grab hold and rush to get it all on camera. Kastle with a K gives me a sardonic wave. Her suit seems to snap crisply as she readies for a live cross, her stitched up throat all but concealed by a silk scarf. The edge of her undead lips turn up, as if she's grinning at me. Grinning like a skull.

The headlines spread like Chinese whispers as I muscle through the cameras, swiping at the flash bulbs. But they don't want me anymore. Journalists, camera men, they move like a startled herd of cows, each one mewling at the others as they race to their vans. They need footage. They need experts. They know what this could mean.

I know what it could mean, too.

I remember when the president went on TV, John Ramsey this was, back when the Newly Dead first appeared. My dad called him *Johnny Death*. You can guess why. Johnny Death talked of tension, that was how he started. He was an old oil man and he talked about the thick, strong pipes that held a rig together, that kept the oil pumping, kept the whole dang foozle of a thing running (his words, not mine). Johnny said those pipes only worked if they all pulled together for the greater good, you see what I'm saying? But sometimes the tension gets too much, he said and I remember him lacing his fingers together then snapping them away like a magician performing a trick. That's where the trouble starts, he said.

I don't know a thing about oil unless it's leaking from my Chevy but the gist of Johnny Death's metaphor is cut and dice. Tension. It's a killer.

And once the rest of the world hears that a person hasn't come back as a necro...well, if God is still up there, he's the only one who knows how bad it's really going to get.

Past the media there's more rubber-neckers, homeless bums, t-shirted slobs, people who have caught sight of the flashing lights and make it their private right to know whatever's going on. I thread my way through them, but a solid chest is in my way.

My way's blocked by a Frankenstein tough, a Newly Dead the size of Arnold Schwarzenegger's corpse. Armani suit tight across a barrel chest, wearing sunglasses at night? In his left ear is one of those radio receivers that look like an I-pod cord but God only knows what music a necro like this would listen to. I'm guessing it ain't Celine Dion.

"I believe the scruffy gentleman wishes to get through, brother," the dead Arnie rumbles.

A living guy standing beside the necro says, "Indeed. It is good to want things."

I do a double take. The two behemoths have the same suit, same glasses, same big-as-Arnie muscles, same radio cord. The pair even has the same face. Twins. The only difference is one's dead and one's living.

The night gets a little trippier, especially when I push past the living mountain and hear glass tinkle under his jacket. Unbelievably there's the faint whiff of chlorine. What's he got under there? The Arnie twins are too big to ask and besides, they're looking down at the pebbly beach where Cherry's body is being put on a gurney. Just more people attracted by the lights. Hampton had said his little girl was studying to be an actress. Guess you got your audience, Cherry.

My Chevy's where I left it but I have to wait for a gaggle of Dead Japanese tourists to cross the street, easy to spot in their bright polyester and backpacks. They're taking photos of everything, hookers, dead drunks, telephone poles, and I have to laugh when they stumble dazedly, tripping over their own feet. Newly Dead are susceptible to bright light, makes them confused. Flashes are to undead what tear gas is to the living. Fucks with their synapses somehow. Trust Dead Japanese to still be taking pictures.

Is there a worst kind of walking corpse? Fucking neccer tourists.

Welcome to America. Land of undead and home of the grave.

Chapter 2
Trouble is My
Business

My old Chevy issues a hitching cough as it lurches away from the curb. There's a satisfying popping when the wheels churn rocks at the news vans.

Cherry had been found by a pair of evening walkers, a living girl and a dead guy. Sorry – Dead American. We have to call them that after the Newly Dead were officially recognized by the Constitution and given the same rights as everyone else. Well, some of the rights. They haven't gotten round to all of them yet. That keeps the lobbyists and protestors busy. I like their slogan: DEAD RIGHTS – SOON ENOUGH YOU'LL NEED THEM TOO. A pretty convincing argument, given the Newly Dead aren't going anywhere. More and more on the streets every day.

I see them now, like most nights. It's not that the Newly Dead can't go out in the day; it's just that many of them choose not to. I wouldn't either if I was a rotting corpse. There was a suspect once, a z-boy done for graffiti tagging that Gannon thought would lead us to a bigger fish, and I asked the z-boy what it was like being a corpse in summer.

"Hell, man," was all he said.

13

Hell. No shit.

As I glide through Lower Manhattan, the city spreads out like a waiting whore, I can't tell the Newly Dead from the living. Every so often you can catch a glimpse of a sown up chest, a patchwork leg, a jaw not hanging right; but most of the corpses keep themselves clean, aesthetic. Rotting must be embarrassing. That old human habit of covering up the bad lingers way after death these days. Hell, there's even ads for necro cosmetic surgery that guarantees you'll live the dead life longer if you look after your skin. And why not? We buy the idea when we're alive, so why not when we're dead? The afterlife is still life. In a way.

Plenty of life on the streets tonight, no matter which way you swing. Near Federal Plaza there's a coven of three undead prostitutes, plying their trade in the steamy night air. Necrophilia is no longer illegal – the abolishment of that particular law passed with surprisingly few nays – and even as my Chevy thrums pass, someone's getting a necro blowjob in the shadows of a nearby alley. Dead flesh fucking. Brr. Reminds me of my ex-wife.

The Closet Skeleton is a corner bar off Washington Square, a jip joint taking up space between a Korean restaurant on one side and a rat of an alley on the other. Maybe someone inside knew Cherry, or knew why she wasn't undead. Shit, there I go again. Dead American. Can get into a lot of trouble nowadays for bigotry. We're all equal in America now. The living and the dead. Yeah right.

I walk into the Skeleton, light a cigarette. Besides the waitress, a girl whose youthful glow seems out of place, the bar is filled with the dead. These types of joints had been doing well in the last few years. Though they had no need for food anymore, or air, or life insurance. Necros could still drink! This had puzzled scientists until they realised the undead still had brain power, which meant they still had brain cells to burn. And, just like the living, the dead get off on burning them.

I get the usual stares – dead eyes all round, you know – and I figure the living barmaid's my best bet. But a couple of young necros are hounding her against the jukebox and some idiot's put *Acky Breaky Heart* on. I hate that fucking song. Almost as much as I hate z-boys.

"C'mon, baby," the biggest of the z-boys drools, cupping the girl's breast through her dress with his yellow sausage fingers. "We celebrating tonight and you gonna celebrate with us, just like old times!" The necro looks like a head wound victim. There's a sawn-up gunshot hole in his buzz shaved skull, the wound bordered by thick, black lined tattoos. The young ones always celebrated their reliving with tattoos. Kind of tribal. Personally I think it looks like shit.

"Ye, ye, yeah," the other z-boy puts in eloquently. This one's a skinny runt, held together by what looks like metal poles. Must have broken his neck at some point. I hope it was recent.

Headshot grabs the barmaid's hand, scattering her tray of glasses to the hardwood floor. "C'mon – you ever had dead dick? Huh? You will, baby, you will."

I've had enough. I walk up behind Headshot, grab him by the arm holding the girl, and twist. This is where the cop training comes in handy and not for the first time I'm glad I paid attention that day in the police academy.

Shattering the top of the jukebox with the necro's fist. The necro screams, his friend screams, and Billy Ray Cyrus sounds like he's drowning: *Accckkkkyyyy...brrrrreeeaaaakkkyyyy...* That gives me a good feeling.

The metal frame necro's too high on formaldehyde dipped joints – gravediggers, they call them on the street – and he doesn't believe what he sees, so I twist Headshot's arm, jamming him deeper into the busted machine. This is the best thing to do with necros. They don't feel pain and you can beat one to a bloody pulp and he'll still be standing, and I've even seen one pick her decapitated head up and put it back on her neck. Creepy. The only way to deal with them is to trap them. Then give them shit.

Headshot's growling so I head butt him in the mouth, feeling the satisfying crunch as several of his tombstone teeth snap. It doesn't hurt him but it makes me feel better.

"You boys need to be more polite," I say.

"FUCK YOU!" Headshot spits.

"That's exactly what I mean!" I force his arm further into the jukebox. That's what's great about these old machines – the wheels may have stopped when *Acky Breaky Heart* did, but the jukebox is full of nice, jagged bits of metal. Just right for snagging dead flesh like a fish on a hook. Headshot howls in frustration. He's trapped.

His friend decides it's time to step in and throws a left at me. It's almost pathetically easy to block. I whip my Beretta out for show and bust the metal head's nose, sending him sprawling on his skinny ass. These z-boys. Worse than street punks. They think being dead gives them an edge but they can't fight to save their afterlives.

"You're a dead man," Headshot spits.

"I think you've got us confused. I'm not the dead one around here."

"Yeah!" skinny friend lurches upright, pointing a gnarled finger at me. "When Grand, Grand, Grandpa finds out who you are, you're dead! A dead m, man, man."

"Linus!" Headshot snaps. "Shut your fucking hole."

Linus closes up tight and my old cop instinct kicks in. Linus here must be talking about Grandpa Hob, Harlem's own undead crime lord. He and I go way back.

Hob used to be legit. Paid his taxes, ran a grocers on Malcolm X Boulevard, went to church and kissed babies.

That was before an undead gangbanger caved in his chest with a baseball bat. He changed when he died. Realised he could give more back to the world then just fresh fruit and over-priced milk. Realised he could make more money selling drugs and undead ass. Now, Grandpa Hob, as he calls himself, is a plague on the streets of New York.

I tried to put him away fourteen times when I was on the force but nothing would stick. Evidence would disappear, witnesses would either recant or never be seen again. Hob used scum like these two necros to stay on the streets. He's been running the z-boys for years, gave them their name (actually renamed each of the z-boys after cartoon characters, can you believe it?) and turned all the underage undead into his own army of snitches and toughs. Clearly ole Hob's standards must have slipped in recent years, though, if he was letting two deadbeats like these into his fold.

Diplomacy has never been my strong suit – I have a tux but it's a rental – and it won't do any good to take these dead boys downtown. They'd be out in an hour and all I would get is shit from my former fellow officers. I've dealt with Grandpa Hob's lawyer in the past, a cutthroat former D.A. turned criminal defender named Brenda Barrett. She could really bust balls. I don't know why I married her.

I'm not in the mood to see her tonight so I decide to cut the z-boys loose. Literally.

"Get me out of here, man!" Headshot wails.

"Okay, okay. Quit your crying," I say, reaching for the knife lying on a recently finished plate of t-bone on a nearby table. You ever seen a steak knife cut through undead flesh? Not pretty.

By the time I finish, Headshot's hand and most of his forearm is a gory mess in the remains of the jukebox, and his ragged stump looks like a badly carved ham. He's thinking about starting it up again – he has that look in those milky eyes of his – but the way I twirl the steak knife, still dripping with his clotty blood, must be enough for him to reconsider.

"C'mon, Charlie, let's g, g, g, get out of here," Linus almost cries, already up and heading for the door. "Don't worry 'bout your arm, g, g, grandpa get you 'nother."

Charlie the Headshot backs away, gives me that look again. Like he can't wait to get me alone. "I ain't worried about my arm, deadshit. Nahuh."

The door doesn't hit them on the way out. The remains of Charlie's arm scramble weakly in the jukebox. It was kind of pointless, what I just did. Newly Dead body parts can act independently of the body – like when a lizard detaches its tail at the first sign of trouble. I saw a scientist explain it once on the news, though he'd used big words and a lot of jargon. Seems dead muscles can connect easier than live ones – just sew the pieces together and the weird shit that makes the dead into undead will keep the corpse together. Doctors tried to harness the chemical reaction or electron surge or whatever it is to help live transplants. It hadn't worked, but it had resulted in a new medicine for the rich Newly Dead who wanted to stay alive (ha ha) forever. Started a massive underground market in dead body parts. People like Grandpa Hob make a mint off it, so I know Charlie can get another arm easy enough.

But I wonder how long it will be before I meet Snoopy and the rest of the Peanuts gang, now that I've taken Charlie Brown's arm. Questions, questions, but I've got no time to come up with answers because the barmaid's all thankyous and smiles. And I love gratitude when it's a girl that's giving it.

She tells me she's had trouble with the z-boys before; nothing major, just the usual shit she takes for working in a neccer bar. Tonight was the first time they'd taken it this far, however. I ask her why and she shrugs.

Says they were talking about looking to party, like they had something to celebrate. She takes me to the bar, pours me a bourbon. The dead patrons holding up the bar turn away and look into the bottom of their glasses. The bourbon glass is clean and I like the place. Here even the dead leave you alone.

The barmaid says her name's Dorothy. She's almost a cliché, black hair in a bob, unblemished skin straight from her daddy's farm in Kansas. I wonder if she has a plaid dress at home and an annoying black dog. She even has rosy cheeks. But she turns pale when I show her the pictures of Cherry.

"Is she...dead?"

I point out the obvious and ask Dorothy if she knows the dead girl. She shakes her head, brown bangs falling across her eyes. Dorothy usually works days, is only filling in tonight – "Customers are more placid in the daytime," she shrugs– but Cyrus would know, Cyrus Beaumont, the owner.

Cyrus. That was one of the names that had come up today when I'd asked around after Cherry. "Ask Cyrus Beaumont," Ready Ronnie Sikes, a Dead Italian had told me at his Soho restaurant. I knew Ronnie from the days when he used to snitch on Dead Irish Americans for the mob, back before Hob made all the Dead Italians and Sicilians put on their own concrete shoes before taking a dip in the East River. I get a strange feeling when I think about all those undead mobsters sitting on the river bottom trying to gnaw themselves free. Kind of like...happiness.

Today, Ready Ronnie had been eating a plate of cannelloni made by his dead mother, though God only knows why since undead don't need to eat. I guess Ready Ronnie does it to feel more human.

"Cyrus runs most of the girls for Hob, picks them up at the Port Authority, Central Station, off the boat or whatever, you know," Ready Ronnie had said, twisting a swirl of pasta with his fork. "Heard he promises to put 'em on Broadway or some shit. Huh. Closest they get to being stars is giving blowjobs backstage at the Shubert. Fergetboutit."

Ready Ronnie forked the mouthful of pasta past his chapped grey lips and I almost gagged. Where did the food go if Newly Dead couldn't eat? A question I'll have to ask Ready Ronnie later because I've got more to ask of Dorothy.

Dorothy says Cyrus is out of town on business. What sort of business? Dorothy doesn't know. When will he be back? Tomorrow morning. I leave her a card and a Death butt in an ashtray. Ask her to tell Cyrus I'll be back in the morning. With some questions.

I knock back my drink. The bourbon burns all the way to the car.

Chapter 3
Vengeance Is Mine

My office. It's a bombsite but it's cleaner than my apartment. I have yet to get around to hiring a maid – I delegate duties a lot. But since I have yet to hire a secretary to delegate to, it's probably moot.

I rent some space in the East Village, above a restaurant in Little India. The smell can get a bit much. Ever been high on curry? It's not good. But the rent's cheap, the landlord doesn't speak English and there's 10% off naan bread for living under his roof.

The first day I moved in – moved in, such a wrong term for a cardboard box of empty folders, a bottle of bourbon and a half dead Japanese peace lily. I noticed there were no necros in Little India, or at least no Dead Indians. The landlord's granddaughter and go-between, a Hindu version of Britney Spears in her Mouseketeer days, told me matter-of-factly that when someone in Little India died they made a pilgrimage to the real India and the holy water of the Ganges. There, they'd cast themselves into the river like the corpses of old and just float away.

When I asked Indian Britney what happened after that, where did they go, she popped her cherry bubblegum and said, "Dunno." Chew. "They don't come back though." Chew. "Like, not ever."

I pour myself a bourbon. Somehow the idea of just

floating away when you die sounded peaceful. Kind of serene. That makes me think of Cherry Hampton drifting in the water off Carl Schurz Park. She didn't look that peaceful.

There's a knock at the door. The mottled glass of the door makes it hard to see who it is, but just above the raised letters of ROTAGITSEVNI ETAVIRP – YADARAF, there's blonde hair haloed by the hallway light. A woman. Either that or it's Fabio. Last I heard he was living the dead life in Morocco, greeting guests at a casino and posing for his next zombie Mills & Boons cover.

I finish my drink in one bolt, light a Death cigarette and tell whoever it is to come in. Normally I don't smoke when I first meet people - sick of all the talk that it will kill me - but I do find that smoking gives off the right image. Everyone expects a PI to smoke. Hate to disappoint.

In walks a dead woman. By the cut of her Gucci jacket she's worth more than a few bucks. Catwalk walk. Blonde hair's a shimmering wave, she must spend thousands to keep it from going grey and stringy like dead hair does. The skin across her cheekbones is tight, youthful. She must be into plastination, the new craze for Newly Dead who want to keep themselves looking young and healthy in their afterlife. Can't tell how she died, no visible wounds. Despite myself, I'm aroused. The Death cigarette smoulders, unsmoked, on my lips.

"Mr Faraday?" she asks, her voice like liquid honey. "I realise it's late but I need your help."

"And how can I help you, Miss...?"

"It's Mrs," she says with a hint of steel. She's giving herself away already. "My name is Evelyn Trask. My husband is Stephen Trask. You may have heard of him?"

Vaguely. Some big-wig in the legal drug community. Worth millions. He farts and the share price wavers. Wears suits that cost more than a necro's annual wage. You know the type. They're the people who walk past you without seeing you. And they always look so fucking happy.

I swallow the metaphorical bile. "I've heard of him. He makes aspirins right?"

She doesn't blink. "You could say that. Stephen works for Omega America, Mr Faraday, and chances are if you've ever had a headache you've taken one of *their* aspirins. But Omega's more than that. Stephen's on the board of directors of one of the largest pharmaceutical companies in the world."

I stare at her. She's expecting more of a reaction. When she doesn't get one, she sniffs and says, "They are quite big. Lots of old money made by old men with their fingers in a lot of pies. Stephen's one of their rising stars. He's worth seven figures. I'm not telling you this to boast, Mr Faraday, merely so you realise who my husband is. Who you will be dealing with."

She perches on the end of my threadbare couch, crosses a pair of perfect legs. Her black stockings make a satisfying sound. She doesn't seem disgusted by her surroundings. Doesn't even raise an eyebrow at the TV dinner coagulating on the seat beside her. She's classy.

"What's he done to you, Mrs Trask?"

"You're astute, Mr Faraday. How did you guess that?"

I shrug. "You wouldn't be here if your husband hadn't done *something* wrong. And since you're here and not at some up-market investigator's office your husband's seven figures could afford, I'm guessing it's something you don't want anyone to know about. No one in your circle, at least."

She smiles tightly, one of those demure beauty queen smiles that doesn't show any teeth. Her eyes are a deep blue from the contact lenses she wears to mask the dead white. "Yes, you're right Mr Faraday. This...*investigation* is not one I would wish known. And I heard you pride yourself on your...discretion."

Do I? Destruction maybe, but discretion? Sure, when I'm on a case I can be confidential. The reason I ask so many questions is because I rarely like to answer them. But discrete? Things always seem to go wrong around me, which makes a lot of noise and causes a lot more damage.

"Who's been spreading stories about me?"

The dead beauty says, "A friend of a friend, Alison Kastle. With a K."

Ah, everyone's favourite undead reporter. I remind myself to thank Kastle for the business next time I see her, and say: "Tell me what I can do for you, Mrs Trask."

She's wearing a scarf even though it's warm out and she pulls at an errant wool thread with a pair of shapely fingernails. She's nervous. She's been dancing around it every since she walked in the door, and now that I'm leading she doesn't know if she likes the moves or not. Or where the dance may take her.

Then she sighs, and says: "My husband...I believe he is having an affair, Mr Faraday. And I wish to know with whom."

Ah. Your standard husband hunt. Easy money. Tracking a stray man is one of the least complicated cases to work. Usually the adulterous husband is lulled from the sex and doesn't suspect anyone would be following him, so he doesn't see the PI. The man thinks the only one to worry about is his wife, and, even more often, he thinks she doesn't suspect a thing. We men are like that most of the time. Smug and wrong.

Still, looking at Evelyn Trask, I wonder if her suspicions might be misplaced. Sure, she's dead, a necro bride. But at least she died in her prime and given how much of her husband's cash she's obviously spent on preservation salons and undead beauty products, there's not a hell of a lot of difference between her now then when she was alive. Most of these uptown girls are half plastic when they're living anyway, so there's not much difference when they're dead. I'm sure her breasts are fake. They look fantastic pushing against her camel hair coat.

But as a wise man once said, show me a beautiful woman and I'll show you a man who's tired of fucking her. Maybe that was it. Maybe even a dead cow at home doesn't stop Trask going out for fresh milk.

"Okay," I say, "What makes you think your husband's having an affair?"

The perfect skin around her eyes scrunches, the closest to an admission of pain a woman like Evelyn Trask will allow to be seen. "At first I thought I was imagining it all. Stephen's been putting in long hours lately, some big deal he's working on that he says will save Omega. You've heard about the company being bought up? No? Well, my husband seems to think he can single-handedly save the company from being taken over. So he's been working a lot. But then little things started to happen. Phone calls he hangs up when I walk in the room. Longer than normal business trips. Strange numbers on his phone bill." Evelyn fluffs at her blonde hair, smoothes it down. "But I suppose the biggest tell is that he doesn't fuck me anymore."

I'm shocked and I must look it. It's not the use of the word – I've got nothing against cursing, no fucking way – but just hearing it come from such a pair of cultured lips is enough to make me bite my tongue.

The dead woman sniffs. "I may look like money, Mr Faraday, but I wasn't always. I grew up in the Bronx and nothing shocks me. Not even dying. Do you know how I died? It was in *all* the papers."

"I only read the horoscopes."

"We were skiing at Aspen when I misjudged the slope. Broke both my legs and most of my ribs, collapsed my lungs and snapped my neck. If I had lived, I never would have walked again. One newspaper called me lucky."

She snorts out a sigh from her pert nose. "I suppose I am. But after that, after all the operations, no matter how they put me back together again, Stephen wouldn't touch me. Wouldn't look at me. Oh, he'd hold my hand when the cameras were flashing, sure. But that was all. I may be a zombie, Mr Faraday, but I'm married to a ghost. A ghost who doesn't like fucking a neccer."

My mind works faster than my manners. "You think he's cheating because you're dead?"

"Yes."

"Why?"

She sidles up to my desk on that great pair of stems. She has the lingering scent of roses. There must be some new way of masking the stench of decomposition I haven't heard about. She smells good. Most necros leave a bad taste in my mouth.

Evelyn Trask slides a piece of newspaper from her purse, lays it on my desk. "I found this in his study. I rang the number. I was told the place specializes in living girls. It's on Canal and Lafayette. Do you know it?"

The scrap's an ad for a brothel called EASTERN BUTTERFLY and the address tells me what to expect. "It's in Chinatown. Looks like a massage parlour with extras, if you get me. But a newspaper doesn't prove anything."

"Exactly, Mr Faraday. That's why I'm here. I want you to follow my husband and find proof that he is cheating." The dead woman's eyes gleam. "Then I can really fuck him."

While I don't normally trust blondes – been double-crossed too many times in the past – her honesty's a turn on and I feel like saying yes right away.

But I still think about it. I don't like taking on two cases at once (even though I always seem to) but this looks like an easy gig. Besides, tomorrow I had to give Hampton back the retainer for Cherry, which meant last month's rent wasn't taken care of and this month's slipped further down the rankings of financial importance. I need the money. Figure I can keep tabs on Stephen Trask while still looking into what happened to Cherry. It shouldn't be too difficult. I agree to take the case.

She gives me one condition. "Whatever you find out, Mr Faraday, you mustn't tell anyone. I may want to ruin my husband but I don't want to destroy him with scandal. I want him to have big earning power for a long time. So I can siphon him dry."

Evelyn Trask has copies of her husband's phone bill, a list of the places he goes and an envelope full of cash. I don't even bother counting it. Wouldn't give her the satisfaction.

"He breakfasts at the Harvard Club most mornings," she says. "Or so he tells me."

The dead broad walks out in a swish of stockings, a sway of perfect hips, a flash of too-white teeth. Stops at the door. "Find me proof, Mr Faraday. And you'll be rewarded. Handsomely."

Never fuck with a dead woman. They live forever and never forget.

Chapter 4
The Twisted Thing

The necro leaves before I can reconsider. I'm a sucker for a dead blonde. Cherry's a dead blonde, too. Only she isn't walking and flirting and plotting revenge like Mrs Stephen Trask. Cherry isn't doing anything at all. Not since someone found a way to put her in the grave permanently.

I try to catch some sleep, figuring there's not much that can be done before dawn on either case.

Dreams. Random, inconsistent images. Cherry in the river, only she's not alone, there are hundreds of versions of her, hundreds upon hundreds of dead, blonde girls just floating in the gentle current. I dream of Evelyn Trask and a massage parlour in Chinatown, and she works there now and she's offering a rub down. I dream of Gannon and Conroy and the z-boys from The Closest Skeleton and even the Arnie twins from the crime scene, all together in a bar in Greenwich shooting glass upon glass of formaldehyde served by a frightened Dorothy.

I dream trippy, lucid dreams that wake me scant hours later, confused, unkempt. The office smells like tandoori. The sun is scratching the horizon. It's time to go to work.

An hour later my Chevy's parked outside the Harvard Club. At least a bad night's sleep meant lighter traffic. Another New York morning.

There's a picture of Stephen Trask on the dashboard. Typical fat cat. Double chin from too much of the good things in life. Piggy eyes. Flabby skin. Looking at him makes you wonder why his wife cares that he doesn't have sex with her anymore. Then again, when you're worth hundreds of millions, who actually cares what you look like? You can always buy love, and maybe Evelyn just wants her husband to spend his cash on her. I'm not paid to ask those sorts of questions so I push the thought aside, light a smoke and keep my eye on the door of the club.

It's not long before he turns up in a black BMW, license plate: TRASK. A dead giveaway. He goes into the club without tipping the necro valet and I sit another thirty minutes until another dead valet – could be the same one, I don't know, they all look the same to me – brings the Beamer back and Trask comes out of the club.

He looks like he had a better breakfast than the half eaten hot dog and lukewarm coffee on my dashboard – I'm guessing you can get a damn good hotdog with a seven figure income – when a dead man comes out behind Trask, talking to him. He's a dead man I know well and seeing him here, so far from Harlem, piques my interest. His name's Randal Hob. But most people call him Grandpa.

What is the CEO of a pharmaceutical giant doing eating breakfast with a necro mobster?

Evelyn Trask's suspicion of her husband's infidelity may be a little way off. Not unless he's fucking Ole Hob. Ugh. Can you imagine that? I don't want to.

The pair talk animatedly enough for me to wish I had brought my long range mic. I curse my lack of forethought but at least I brought my camera. I take a few shots of the pair before the conversation ends and Trask steps into his Beamer.

A smooth, black Lincoln pulls up behind Trask and a necro tough in a tight suit jumps out and opens the door for Hob. He's a smart old corpse. Never seen in public with his more unruly z-boys, his bodyguard today looks like your standard undead bullet-taker. Wouldn't turn a head in this part of town, where most personal security are Newly Dead. And why not? You can pay them less thanks to the necro minimum wage, they never sleep, and they don't steal from your refrigerator. And bullets just go right through them.

Trask pulls out into traffic and I wait until Hob's Lincoln slides in behind him before I gun my Chevy. Hob turns north towards Rockefeller Centre, no doubt heading back to his hiding hole in Harlem, while Trask takes a left heading south down 6th Avenue. From the dossier his wife gave me, Trask has an office on Wall Street. But Chinatown's south, too. Maybe Stephen Trask's off to see some eastern butterflies. I follow.

The traffic's turned heavy already. Most of the trip finds me sandwiched between yellow taxis milling at the lights like impatient sprinters. The taxi drivers are all necros, Dead Sikhs and Dead Iranians and a couple of Dead Jamaicans, their grey dreadlocks creepy messes of grey hair like bloated spiderwebs. Reminds why I still like to drive myself in this city.

Trask's BMW is three cars ahead. Soon enough he takes a turn onto Canal Street and I know he's heading for Lafayette. This could be the quickest money I've ever made.

Eastern Butterfly is between an alleyway and a dry cleaner. The outside's nondescript, your typical weathered green stone, drab compared to the multi-coloured lanterns and red banners strung across the top of the street. Not a very high class joint. Trask could afford a hundred times more to get his rocks off. So why come here? I'm guessing it's for the same reason Evelyn Trask hired me. To keep it low key. Either that or Eastern Butterfly was more than just your average sex parlour and Trask was looking for something dirtier, darker, and closer to the streets than a penthouse with a $10,000 hooker. Something you can only buy in Chinatown, not uptown.

Trask finds a park out front but I have to circle the block a few times before a tiny Dead Chinese man moves a delivery van and I can park. Lucky Mrs Trask gave me the newspaper ad or it would be hard to pick up Trask's trail.

Chinatown smells like dead fish and week-old noodles. Most of the people on the streets are Newly Dead Orientals or second and third generation Dead Chinese Americans, but there's also a scattering of your plain whites, living and dead.

I pass a group of fat, dead men playing mah jong on a rickety table, and I catch a snippet of the news coming from their tinny transistor radio:

...ile the NYPD have yet to issue an
official statement, initial reports confirm
that the young woman did not relive,
making her the first person in two decades
not to come back as Newly Dead. Life
supremacist groups are already
proclaiming the news a godsend, while
dead rights organisations are concerned
with the implications this will have on
New York's estimated four million
undead. Dr Tanya Lacy, prominent
Newly Dead activist and academic, said
the news has many Dead Americans
worried for the future. "We want to
know how she didn't relive and why, and
we want to know now. There's a lot of
fear on the streets of New York today...

The old necros playing mah jong don't seem to hear the radio, they're too intent on their tiles. Ignorance transcends death. Then again, I look around and everything seems normal. There must be a lot of fear elsewhere. Yet I don't blame the lobbyists for coming out at the news. The first truly dead person in twenty years would make any necro worry.

New Yorkers have gotten secure in their afterlife; nowadays they live as if they know they have years left after they die, and they do. No matter what happens in your life, death doesn't hold any mysteries anymore. But now that Cherry's dead, the afterlife doesn't look so rosy. Maybe whatever it is that keeps the corpses out of their graves has worn off. Maybe we're all going to die for real now. Maybe there's more room in Hell.

I shake off the thought, try to focus on the task at hand. Stephen Trask diddling Asian girls on the side. Right.

Game face on, it's time to use some of that discretion I'm supposedly known for and forgo the front door. There's an alleyway beside the massage parlour that looks all but deserted. There's the back of a restaurant at the end and a white clad busboy, a Dead Korean by the look of it, throwing rotten lettuce into a Dumpster. Above, those ubiquitous red lanterns hang from fire escapes and drain pipes, dozens of them, like strings of crimson pearls. Grimy, brick gardens of low cut green are spaced along the walls, giving the place a grassy smell. There are doors with signs for back alley lawyers, cut rate taxidermists and the loading bays of noodle bars. I'm alone except for the busboy at the end.

Eastern Butterfly's on my right and I run my hand along the brick as I saunter down, looking for a window, a door, something to jimmy to get inside. A window boarded with wood. Tight, when I try to pry it. Figures. If the massage parlour is a brothel, they wouldn't want to give out free shows to the neighbourhood boys. Not even an outside lock to pick.

It takes a minute to spot the grated window of a basement behind some rotting boxes. The bars on the window are so rusted they're almost the same tint of shit as the walls of the alley. Rubbing the glass doesn't help see inside. Dark. Even if I get the grate open, it's a tight fit. I wish I'd done some stomach crunches this morning.

I ball the sleeve of my jacket, punch out the glass. The break is muffled. A moment passes and there's no sound from inside, the bus boy doesn't look up. Easy.

The grate's another story. Metal, padlock the size of a grapefruit. Shooting it off would save time but it's probably not the best of ideas. Covert is what I want. I'll have to pick the lock. It takes me longer then I would have thought – I'm rusty, sure, but it's a big lock, give me a break – but soon enough I'm in.

The basement's large but cramped, stacked with mouldy boxes, old suitcases, broken furniture. Stairs lead up, light shining around the edges of a door. It's not locked.

A hallway. Grey carpet, cream walls. Doorways strung with curtains line the hall. The sounds of pleasure coming from within. A whole lot of massaging is going on, I'm sure.

The curtains are flimsy, easy to peek around. Behind them are men's ass cheeks being kneaded by waifish Asian girls, a Japanese man getting a handjob, a fat guy all but smothering a girl as he ruts on top of her like a beached whale heading for water. Nice. This is what I love about my job. The colourful characters you get to meet. At least Mrs Trask will be happy to know she wasn't lied to. All the girls are alive at the Eastern Butterfly.

No sign of Stephen Trask behind any of the curtains. He must have paid for one of the more private rooms that actually have a door. There are two at the end of the hallway, close to another hall that, judging from where I came in, must lead to the front of the brothel. I hunker down at the first door, look through the key hole. The room's dark, empty. Must be a slow day. But there's pay dirt at the other keyhole.

The room looks bathed in blood from the sunlight coming through a red curtain. Trask is lying naked on a bed. There's someone beside him on the bed but the light and his bulk cover whoever it is, just the hint of hair, a thin leg beside Trask's blubbery thigh. Trask is leaning over, whispering something that's too low to hear.

I pull out my camera and thumb off the auto flash, take a photo through the keyhole, then check the digital display. No good. It doesn't even look like Trask, and the girl's just a shadow. I won't get paid for that.

I'm wondering whether to try the old 'housekeeping' trick – and whether or not these rooms even get serviced – when a Dead Thai woman rounds the corner and takes the dilemma out of my hands.

"Hey! You! Hey!"

She's clearly got a way with words but even if her extensive vocabulary doesn't draw attention, the screaming will. Covert's had its day and discretion is done, so I click the flash back on the camera and take a shot of the Dead Thai to shut her up. The light disorientates her, makes her stagger like a drunk. Buys me enough time to kick the door in.

"Housekeeping!" I cry, slamming into Trask's room and working the camera.

The flash strobes, painting the room in white moments. There's Trask, one hand held up to the camera, the other over his groin. A small chest pressed against some impressive man-tits. A great white ass pocked with pimples, lumbering into frame as he grasps for his pants. The figure on the bed, sweat stained sheet pulled up around them, the skin shiny for some reason, as if the camera were shooting glass.

Trask hollers inarticulately as he struggles to put his shirt on. But I can't take my eyes – or the camera – off the person on the bed. The camera whirrs, taking shot after shot as I stare at the person Stephen Trask came here to fuck.

It's not a living girl, like his wife feared. It's a boy. A dead boy.

And young, too, he must have only been ten or eleven when he died. Someone's put some money into him by the looks. His embalming job is surprisingly good given the locale, making his skin glossy, youthful. He looks Thai, too. A little, Dead Thai boy.

Fuck. I wonder what Evelyn Trask will think of this.

Her husband is stumbling around the room, throwing wads of money at me as he tries to get into his pants, pleading and threatening in the same breathe.

I can't stand looking at the little zombie boy anymore, and the scene makes me think of Gray Gary J. I don't want to think about that. It's time to get out of there.

I head for the doorway, stumble through. Startled prostitutes and Johns stare at me from behind their curtains. The Dead Thai woman in the hall is gone, probably to round up the Eastern Butterfly's equivalent of security. The basement door is closed.

A minute later I'm breathing the stale air of the alleyway and running for my Chevy, the camera a dead weight in my hand. The pictures will almost certainly ruin the Trasks' marriage, give Mrs the leverage over Mr. I'll get paid, Evelyn Trask will get paid, and Stephen Trask will be the one doing the paying. I should be happy.

But all I can think about is that little dead boy and the hell of a world he died into.

Chapter 5
Finger Man

The McDonald's near Freedom Plaza is still being picketed. The protesters first hit the street two weeks ago and today their banners are still in the way when I jaywalk. The protest signs look like taglines from B grade horror flicks: A ZOMBIE STOLE MY JOB, DEAD PEOPLE MAKE YOUR BURGERS and YOU WANT DEATH WITH THAT? The picketers are hard faced living adolescents sweating in their sandwich boards, but their resolution after a fortnight is astounding. Not that you can blame them. If a necro stole my job I'd be pissed too.

One girl with a roadmap of acne on her cheeks is screaming something into a megaphone. She's too loud to discern the words. I don't know if it's the static or her spit that keeps the early morning walkers passing by. Unfortunately, the other picketers are easier to understand.

"A corpse cooked your fries!" a black haired slob hollers in my face.

"The dead belong in graves, not in your service!"

"Jobs are for the living!"

I long for the days when meat was murder but soon enough the picketers are behind me, harassing a pair of elderly women walking a shih tzu. By the looks of the old women it won't be long until they shuffle from this mortal coil themselves. The protestors should leave them alone. That's almost discrimination these days.

I push through the cheery glass and step into the frosty air of the McDonald's. Soulless, tuneless muzak buzzes my ear. Crime scene Conroy's at a back table, right where his office said he'd be.

I really should have called Evelyn Trask, handed over the photos of her husband and collected my money before trying to find Conroy. But the face of that little Dead Thai boy burns behind my eyes and I don't want to look at the photos yet, don't want to hand them over. Talking to Conroy about Cherry will take my mind off it. Swap one dead girl for another. Why not? They're a dime a dozen nowadays, especially in McDonald's.

Behind the counter, undead serve up mushy burgers and burnt fries, the sharp tang of salt and fat covering the reek of their dead skin. Ronald McDonald got a lot of flak for laying off his living employees and hiring Newly Dead. The papers called it a major victory for Dead Rights. The living lobbyists called it the most blatant desecration of workplace relations since slavery. I think they're being melodramatic. Then again, I'm not the one complaining about losing a job in front of a fryer.

Conroy is pushing a sad looking pickle around his tray when I take a seat across from him. He jumps when he sees me. Skittish this morning. Maybe I'm not the only one who had a bad night's sleep.

"Faraday? What are you doing here?"

"I called the morgue. They said I'd find you here. I don't get it, Conroy – why come all the way here for lunch? There's more Mickey Ds than taxi cabs in New York, surely there must be one closer to Police Plaza."

Conroy looks away and I follow his stare. A necro girl, probably sixteen the time she died, is manning the nearest register. Her hair is plaited like Heidi and a flap of her face must have come away, since a row of staples make a garish crescent on her cheek. McDonald's would have hired her because of the new minimum wage – necros don't need what the living do, so they could afford to make less .

I can guess why Conroy's looking at her. She would have been cute before she died.

The forensic pathologist flushes red. "Good burgers, that's all," he says, looking down at his half finished quarter pounder.

"Right. So. Tell me about the dead girl."

"She's just a friend, you know, I mean, it's not like it's illegal, I mean, technically she's twenty-five even though she only looks fifteen, she died, like, ten years ago..."

"Conroy, I'm not talking about your neccer crush. I meant the girl you fished out of the river last night. Cheryl Hampton."

He seems relieved, enough to stop pushing that goddamn pickle around, but only for a moment. Something steels inside him. "Gannon would have my ass if he knew I was talking to you."

"I won't tell if you won't."

"Yeah, but..."

"I just want to know the cause of death. You said last night you'd have a better idea in the morning. You don't want her father to be misinformed, do you?"

"No, but..."

"Then just tell me."

"I can't..."

"Well, then I can't believe what I'm about to do."

I stand up and take a step, making it seem to Conroy that I'm about to place an order with his little neccer girl. "You think Heidi over there's into necrophilia paedophilia? What am I saying? I'll just go and ask her."

I'm halfway to the counter when Conroy's chair

scrapes the linoleum. "Faraday! Don't!"

"What? You want fries, too?"

"Please!"

I stop. Wait. Conroy is a quivering mess, his moustache a tremor on his lip. I would never have thought he was susceptible to this schoolyard shit but clearly he is. He's not saying anything, though.

"Well?"

He slumps back in his chair, face slack. "Okay. Fine. Just...just come and sit down, okay?"

Conroy looks beaten. He's going to tell me how Cherry Hampton died. From the looks of things, I need to pay attention.

"That laceration you saw on her forehead was sustained post mortem," he says. "It's likely she didn't wash up there but was dumped. There. I told you."

I'm not letting him off that easy. "What makes you think she was dumped?"

Conroy sighs. Clearly he was hoping the scrap of information would be enough. But he should know by now that I need a bigger slab of meat before I leave the table.

"There wasn't enough water in her lungs to suggest she drowned," he says, "nor that she'd been there long. Detective Gannon seems to think she was dumped well after she died."

"So – how did she die?"

"Overdose."

Not what I was expecting, yet an overdose makes sense. Why else would she run away from her daddy's apartment with Central Park views if she wasn't tasting the different life? Cherry's father had called her, "A good girl, she would never..." but Papa Hampton had failed to finish the sentence. She would never smoke crack, Mr H.? She would never leave you? She would never hang out with unsavoury types like the undead junkies you see from your God-like view of the world? Maybe little Cherry did all three and that was why she was dead.

"I can see the wheels in your head turning, Faraday," Conroy sighs again, attention back on the pickle. "And before you ask, she overdosed from a type of drug unknown."

"Your grammar's as bad as your breakfast," I say. "What do you mean *type unknown?*"

"Exactly that. She overdosed – I found her system choked with a narcotic substance, but all tests have failed to reveal what drug it actually is. I initially thought it was a barbiturate, but no. I tested for heroin, cocaine – she had some in her blood, but not enough to kill her – hell I even checked for date rape drugs, Prozac, steroids. Nada. Whatever killed her...it's nothing we've seen before."

Detective Gannon must be having a cat. He always liked quick police work, quick arrests, quick confessions. If the pathology boys didn't know what killed Cherry Hampton then Gannon wasn't likely to close the case any time soon. And that meant he'd be even more pissed off then he was last night. I have to pay him a visit when I can. Just to rub it in.

"So she had, what, heroin and crack, in her system as well?"

He chews half-heartedly on a sad looking burger. "Yeah, some alcohol, cannabis too, but not as much as the other substance. Party girl, so maybe the unknown substance is something new on the streets. I sent a sample to the F.D.A. for analysis." Conroy ropes a soggy fry across his dry lips, eyes straying to the necro Heidi in the paper hat. "Results should be back this afternoon."

"Call me when it comes in?"

Conroy grunts – his way of neither saying yes or no – and I go to leave. But Conroy's still looking at the undead girl and I just can't leave it alone.

"Hey – since you've done me a solid, I'm going to

repay the favour."

Conroy's eyes bug out when he sees me heading for the counter. He's choking on his fries but I just wave back at him. "No need to thank me."

I walk up to the necro girl. The staples in her cheek are like some new millennium piercing and her too-white eyes are bored.

"Welcome to McDonald's, may I take your order?" A tag reading: MY NAME IS TRAINEE is tacked across a shrunken breast and my nose wrinkles at the amount of perfume she uses to mask her decomposition. Again I'm struck by how Conroy, let alone any living man, could be attracted to a necro. To me, even the ones who get breast implants still look exactly like what they are – walking corpses. Then I remember Evelyn Trask, and maybe Conroy's got a point after all.

I order an apple pie, a Coke and some cookies. While the young necro's getting my order, I take the placemat off a nearby tray and write down the number of a Newly Dead who lives in my neighbourhood. Lady Macabre is what he calls himself nowadays, but I knew him when he was just Tony Babalino, a wetback who used to snitch for me when I worked Vice. Tony got capped for a sour deal – ripping off z-boys can be hazardous to your health – and when Tony reanimated he ditched his name and his sex to be who he always wanted to be. An undead transvestite available for weddings, parties and handjobs. Hey, who am I to judge? When I was young I wanted to be Mr T.

Dead Heidi's back with my order and I hand her a pen and ask if she wouldn't mind writing down her name, console number and the store manager's name, since I'm a mystery shopper hired by Mr McDonald to test the response rate of workers to their customers. She looks scared when I mention how the results of the analysis could be detrimental to her future employment prospects with McDonald's, but she's relieved when I say she has nothing to worry about, that her service was friendly and prompt, and that I was really looking forward to having one of the cookies.

While she's writing down her details, I look over at Conroy. He has an eyebrow raised and you can almost smell his nervous sweat from here. I give him a wink.

Dead Heidi wishes me a great day and I head back to the table, slipping her details into my pocket and pulling out Lady Macabre's.

I wave the slip of paper at Conroy and he snatches at it like a pecking pigeon. He opens his mouth but nothing comes out. "I'll wait for your call," I say as I hand him Lady Macabre's number. Macabre would like Conroy. He's into shy guys.

"You got it," Conroy says too quickly, his tongue darting across his lips. "Hey – thanks Faraday."

I can't hide my smile. "Don't mention it."

I leave Conroy to his fantasies and head outside. There. That ought to guarantee Conroy will tell me what the F.D.A. says about the drug in Cherry's system. An unknown drug. Unknown. There's a lot of shit on the streets these days. Cocktails of cocaine and formalin, marijuana soaked in embalming juice, ice cut with chemicals that would kill a living man but get the dead higher than kites. Something for everyone, living or dead. But what's so new on the streets the cops haven't heard of it? And who can I ask about it?

There's something going on outside the McDonald's. The picketers mill together like a pack of rabid dogs, hitting and kicking at something at their feet that I can't make out.

The acne scarred girl stands to the side watching the grim spectacle, the megaphone tight at her mouth. She's screaming again, her face bright red. I catch words like "living" and "neccer" and not much else.

The picketers are beating someone. There's an arm beneath their stamping legs. A dead arm.

One protestor brings his sign swinging down in a wide arc, parting the mob. I lock eyes with a necro teenager they're beating on. A Dead Puerto Rican, maybe a second generation American-born. Couldn't have been more than sixteen when he died. The boy looks scared. But necros don't feel pain. Do they?

I can't watch anymore. Not because he's getting beat. Because I don't feel anything for him. For *it*. Not since Gray Gary J.

There's a meaty chunk when the protest sign hits the boy's face and then the necro boy is lost beneath the trampling of the picketers.

The necro boy calls for help, a pathetic, mewling sound.

Someone should do something.

Chapter 6
Kiss Me Deadly

Police Plaza is only a few blocks away, a left up Gold will get me there. But my Chevy sits idle. I do want to see Gannon, though not to rile him. If I catch him in a good mood (which is very rare) he may give me some idea of what he's found out about Cherry's death (which is probably nada). But you never know. I worked with the brute for years and despite his bull head he's good police. He'll be on the case, just like me. He'll be looking for answers, too. He's a cop first and an asshole second.

Speaking of ass. I need to put aside at least one of the dead girls in my head, so I place a call to Evelyn Trask.

She picks up after one ring. Spooky. I tell her I have something to show her. Her voice is cold as she tells me an address for an apartment near Battery Park. She's either unimpressed by my fast work or she thinks she knows exactly what I'm bringing her. She's in for a surprise.

Thirty minutes later I'm sitting on a twentieth floor balcony overlooking the Hudson, watching Evelyn Trask as she flips through the images on my camera and feeling like a hypocrite for how disgusted I was in Conroy and his necro crush. Mrs Trask looks good, her blonde hair piled high, her throat tanned and smooth. What are they giving necros nowadays? Even embalmed, they look better than living women.

44

Evelyn stops. She sees the pictures of the dead boy. "Is he...?" she asks.

"I'm sorry to be the one to tell you...but yes. The boy...he's Newly Dead."

You have to hand it to upper-class women. They hide themselves well. Except for a tic in her cheek, there's no emotion, no change in Evelyn Trask. I could have just said it was raining outside, for all that she gives away.

"Are there copies, Mr Faraday?"

"Only what's in the camera. I didn't get prints. I knew you wanted to be...discrete."

"Yes." Her voice is flinty. "Discretion is the wisest course of action." She turns her blue eyes away from the camera and onto me. "I suspect you want your money, Mr Faraday? Now that your work is done. Would you give me a minute?"

"Sure. You're buying, so take two."

She slips inside, takes my camera with her. For what she's paying, she can keep it.

I shuck a Death from the packet in my pocket, light it. From the balcony there's a pretty good view of parkland, the river, the Statue of Liberty off in the distance. There are two million immigrants living in New York City and more than half of them are Newly Dead. They come here because they dream the American dream. When they get here, they just end up joining our nightmare. It's worse for the dead ones. No work, high rent, lifism hiding in every nook and cranny. Give me your tired and poor, your huddled masses, hey? Yeah. As long as they're living. The sign on the green lady doesn't say BRING OUT YOUR DEAD.

Evelyn's been gone a while and the view's stopped looking good so I step back into the apartment. The place is tasteful, not too flashy, almost understated really. The rooms don't looked lived in. The Trasks probably own a few properties around town and Evelyn actually lives somewhere else. Then again, given how much money she has, this could be her Tuesday apartment for all I know.

Rich people. Living or dead, they really are different.

I call out, receive a muffled reply from one of the rooms. I'm about to make a joke about how much money she must be paying me, given how long it takes to count it, when I push open the door to find Evelyn Trask sitting on the edge of the bed. Naked. Her, not the bed.

"Let me ask you something," she says, crossing a shapely leg and sliding on a black stocking. "Do you find me attractive?"

"Mrs Trask," I say, "are you trying to seduce me?"

The dead woman laughs bitterly. "I must be rusty if you have to ask." She pulls up the stocking, smoothes it with her palm. She takes a long drag from a menthol smouldering in a clear ashtray beside her. There's an opened bottle of Scotch on the bedside table. The ice in her glass cracks when she takes a sip. It's early for a drink but I was the bearer of bad news. Besides, a beautiful dead woman can take a drink any time of the day she wants to. Especially when she's naked.

"I thought you were getting my money." It's hot in the room and even though my mind's screaming that what's in front of me is a necro, a stinking, rotting corpse, my eyes see something else. A woman, fine, refined, elegant. Made firm by salad lunches and palates when she lived and rebuilt by plastic surgeons and silicone when she died. A luscious woman. A discarded woman. A woman desperate to get back at a cheating husband. And I wonder: is there any better kind of woman?

She lies back on the bed giving me a clear view of heaven. "You'll get your money, Mr Faraday. First, let's talk about your bonus..."

God I love my job.

It's not the first time I've had sex with a dead

woman. One drunken night, a short while after my and Brenda's divorce, I bedded Kastle with a K. And she's never let me live it down. But this...this is different.

Evelyn Trask fucks like a woman who knows that it's fleeting. She knows exactly what this is, and exactly what it can't be, or won't be. She's not doing this to get back at her husband; she's trying to capture something she thought was out of reach or lost to her forever. Sex is like that for women. Deep, soulful. It has meaning. For me, it means getting off. Cold skin or not.

Later, the dead woman smokes a menthol while I put on my pants. The air is sickly sweet when she exhales. I have a vague notion that I've just done something wrong. But like most men the feeling's tempered by the fact I just got laid.

Evelyn opens the drawer of the bedside table, pulls out a thick envelope. She tosses it to me. "Here. Your payment. Cash, of course. And I don't have to ask you to keep this between us, do I, Mr Faraday? You do understand."

She's not asking, she's telling. I nod. Sure.

I'm dressed and thinking about heading out the door when the expression on her face stops me. Nobody could mistake Evelyn Trask for being stupid, despite her body. She looks like a shark. A scheming shark.

"What are you going to do?" I ask.

She doesn't answer for a moment. Her faux blue eyes stare at the smoke trail wafting from the end of her cigarette. I see hate there.

Then she says, "I'm going to have lunch with my husband..." and I know she's not thinking of the salmon salad nicoise at Rafaela's. Hell hath no fury like a dead woman scorned. "Actually, Mr Faraday – would you care to join us?"

God no. "I don't think so, Mrs Trask..."

"I insist. I'll pay you more, if that's what it takes. I

want you there, Mr Faraday, when I show Stephen the photographs. So he can't disprove them. He...he has a way, you see. A way of talking me out of things..."

The door is like a lifeboat on a sinking ship and I want to jump for it. But she grasps my arm tightly and pushes another envelope of money into my hand. Why does she have two ready-made envelopes of cash? Was the plan all along for me to go with her and she knew she'd need more Benjamins for me to agree? Or was she going to pay me to do something else?

The money feels too good in my hand. I'm a glutton for punishment. "Let's do lunch," I say.

Twenty minutes later I'm sitting in a Tribeca bistro named VANITIES, surrounded by power lunching businessmen and rich necro women knocking back Manhattans. A pair of Harvard types at a side table is giving me hot stares. I wish I'd worn a better shirt.

Evelyn Trask sips a mineral water and ignores me. She keeps crossing and re-crossing her legs. Somehow the movement isn't as seductive as it was in my office. My camera is in the centre of the table next to her Dolce purse, and every few seconds the hand not holding her drink strays towards it as if she were afraid the evidence was going to get up and walk out the door.

I'm thinking of doing exactly that when a familiar face stops at the bar. Stephen Trask. He looks different without his arms wrapped around a dead boy.

Trask smiles affably at someone he passes, laughs at a joke, just another suit out for lunch. That is until he sees his wife and the dishevelled bum sitting beside her at table nine. The smile turns upside down by the time he reaches our table.

"Evelyn? Honey, who is this?"

A waiter decides this is the perfect time to serve the bruschetta Evelyn ordered ten minutes ago. Smells good. Probably be in bad taste to eat it, given the circumstances. I grab a piece and eat quickly.

"I have a surprise for you, Stephen," the dead woman says, reaching towards the middle of the table.

Trask squints at me, recognition slowly dawning on his sluggish face. Even with a camera flashing in his face he shouldn't have too much trouble remembering the guy who snapped him in a love-lock with a little dead boy. Something like that stays with a man.

I try to give Trask a reassuring smile but it probably looks strange around a mouthful of bread and tomato. His eyes widen. He knows who I am.

Since he's looking at me, Trask doesn't see the silver handgun that Evelyn pulls from her purse, or the shaky way she cocks the hammer. He does hear the click though.

His eyes dart to his wife. "What...*what* is this?"

Evelyn is fierce, as if holding the gun has somehow unlocked years of hatred, and self-loathing, and regret. She stands up lithely, kicks back her chair. She aims the gun squarely at her husband's face.

Trask is obviously as surprised as everyone else. The diners around us pull back with strangled shouts of alarm. Everyone sees the gun now and no one knows what to do. Neither do I.

"Mr Faraday?" she asks silkily. "Would you be so kind as to tell my husband what *this* is?"

I'm tempted to say *a lunch date* but sarcasm has its place and I figure it's not at table nine at Vanities right this moment. I go with the obvious: my cardinal rule is never lie to an armed woman. "A gun?"

"Exactly," she says.

Trask opens his mouth. "Evelyn, what do you think you're d-"

Boom.

Trask's forehead explodes, splattering the man sitting behind him with blood and meat and brain. He screams, clawing at the gore with a napkin, and it starts a stampede in the restaurant. People knock over chairs, scrambling to get out, kicking each other to get away from the mad woman with the gun.

Trask flops face down in the bruschetta. Damn. I was hoping for another slice.

For a second I think Evelyn Trask is going to turn the gun on me – her husband's not the only man who fucked her in her afterlife – but then she calmly puts the little pistol on the table, smoke still trailing from the barrel, and sits down. Except for the dead body, it's like the whole thing never happened, she's that calm.

"I couldn't let him talk," Evelyn Trask says as she takes a sip of mineral water.

She says nothing else. Neither do I. What can really be said at a moment like this? *Check please?* I'm crass but I do have my limits.

A while later I'm watching a pair of blues put my ex-client in handcuffs. One of the uniforms puts his hand on her head and ushers her into the back of a black and white. She must pay a mint for that hair. It doesn't even ruffle.

Gannon must be busy fucking my ex-wife, as it's Detective Madeline Lopez who's standing beside me at this particular crime scene, notebook open. I know Lopez from my days on the beat. She's one of the few who treat me professionally now and not like some leper that must be avoided.

"It's a clear cut case," she says.

"The bruschetta?" I ask.

"Impounded as evidence, I'm afraid."

My evening's ruined.

Evelyn Trask stares into space from the back of the

police car. Her face is unreadable. She's taken away in a swirl of flashing lights. The two envelopes of money are a dead weight against my chest.

Now I know what the second envelope was for. She wanted to pay me to kill her husband. The extra cash was for a hit. But when she saw the photographs of him and the dead boy, something must have snapped. She must have wanted to do it herself. Hell definitely has no fury.

A pair of paramedics is wheeling the corpse of Stephen Trask on a gurney and he relives just outside the door. He almost knocks out one of the meds trying to load him in the back of an ambulance. The look on what's left of Trask's face is priceless. Shame his wife didn't get to see it.

Lopez says, "I don't need any more from you, Faraday. Just don't leave town."

Why would I leave? New York's a hell of a town.

Chapter 7
Black Alley

America's first dead girl in twenty years haunts my
thoughts. Her blonde hair is on every street corner, her
cherubic lips on every face, her coltish legs in every pair of
jeans on Broadway. Why didn't she relive like Trask just
did? What is it about Cherry Hampton, snob country club
girl turned New York runaway, that makes her so special?
Why wasn't there a dead girl knocking on the Hampton's
door last night instead of a cop with bad news?

I hate questions, generally because the answers
hound me. I have to know. Probably why private
investigation was so appealing when the force kicked me
out. So I could get paid to find answers.

I have an appointment to see Douglas Hampton III
in about an hour. In truth, I wasn't looking forward to
seeing Cherry's father. He'd hired me a week ago to find
her. The next time I saw him I expected to have a girl in
one hand and a cheque (from him) in the other. Now that
Cherry was dead – the first person in America, probably
the world, not to reanimate – I didn't know what Hampton
wanted of me. But when I called last night he'd requested
a meeting. Maybe there was a part of the case he wasn't
sure of. Just like me.

I figure there's enough time to see Cyrus at The
Closet Skeleton before spending thirty odd minutes in
traffic to get to Hampton's Dakota Building apartment.
Putting off the inevitable is easier when the world's like

this. Everything's inevitable, so there's no point sweating it.

The Closet Skeleton is closed. At least it looks closed, until two familiar-looking toughs step out the front door, smoke trailing at their heels. It takes a moment to register where I know them from before it hits me like a dead fish – the two suits from last night at Carl Schulz Park where Cherry was found. The Arnie twins.

I've told you about my cop instinct. It always gets me into trouble and today is no different. There's smoke coming from beneath the door of the Skeleton and I want to know why. Before I know what I'm doing, I'm out of my Chevy and hollering at the twins.

The dead Arnie twin stops, starts to turn like a lumbering dinosaur. Living Arnie is faster. He had seemed further down the street, but before I have a chance to bullshit he's within swinging distance. Actually, he's a lot closer than swinging distance now that he's hit me and knocked me on my ass.

Twittering birds are suddenly everywhere and my head feels raw. At least the pavement against the back of my skull is cool.

Hunkering down, living Arnie bunches my shirt in his ham-sized fist and hauls me up. I can't focus as he pushed me backwards. Scrabbling at his fingers doesn't even scratch him. When the sun dips behind a building, it dawns on me that I'm being dragged into an alley. Great. I hate alleys.

"Curiosity killed the cat, didn't it, Dutch?" Living Arnie says.

"Indeed it did, Butch," Dead Arnie – Dutch – rumbles. "Or was it you that killed the cat?"

"Or you?"

"I can never remember either."

The back of my head hits a Dumpster and it's almost a relief when Butch lets go. Those damn birds are still flying in front of my eyes, but all swiping at them does is topple me over.

Undead Dutch puts a boot against my chest. The cuffs of his pants are singed, like he'd been stepping through fire. My nose is ripe with the smell of charred skin and chlorine, the same sourness I smelt on his brother last night. What – have they been starting fires in swimming pools?

There's blood in my mouth, running from a gash above my left eye from when my forehead got in the way of Butch's fist. I spit out blood in a cough.

"I believe you hit him too hard, brother."

"Nonsense. A slap, nothing more."

"Hmm." Dutch's corpse breath reeks as he picks me up and pushes me against the Dumpster. The wire from the white-corded radio in his ear is dangling in front of a ragged hole in his cheek, yellowed teeth poking out from reeking darkness. Those teeth were due for a brush about a year ago.

I try to run. I can't. I try to talk. I can't. My face is hot with blood. My gun's in my shoulder holster but it seems too far away, too much effort to draw right now. There's a fire escape above me, strapped to the wall of the Skeleton and mocking me with its safety and distance.

The living one puts a finger to the receiver in his ear, cocks his head as he listens. "The gentleman wants to know his name."

Dutch pats me down, taking out my wallet, my cell phone, the wads of money from Evelyn Trask. A bone white hand goes into my jacket and pulls out my Beretta. There's not much else for me to do except sit here.

"I have his gun, brother o' mine."

"Excellent."

The big corpse puts my things in his jacket, flips open my wallet. "Jon Faraday is his name."

Butch relays this to his cuff link. He squints as he

listens. Then he says, "Copy." to the transmitter at his wrist.

He bends down. Finally my eyes can focus and I don't like what I see – myself reflected in the mountain's Raybans, blood splattering my face like arterial spray and a vaguely stupefied look in my eyes. Not my finest hour.

"I believe he is still conscious, Butch."

"Not for long, Dutch."

Then all I see is fist.

And blackness.

All too soon a voice cuts through the dark: "You want to tell me what you're doing at another one of my crime scenes, *Faraday?*"

Groan. I think it's my mother talking and I want to tell her no, five more minutes, please I don't want to go to cop school today – I'm a little bit out of it, if you can't tell – but then I realise that my mother's in a Newly Dead retirement home in Alaska, that I haven't been to the police academy for twenty years, and there's no way my mother, dead or living, would ever call me *Faraday*. Especially not in that tone.

"Why does everyone keep asking me that?" I say, struggling to stand. My face feels like mashed potato and I'm breathing blood. My shirt front is a red mess. Great. I just bought this shirt last year.

"Because you're always in the wrong place, Faraday."

I finally look up and there's Detective Ray Gannon, no less pissed then when I saw him last night. Actually, he looks more pissed if that's possible. Behind him there are lights, a patrolmen putting up yellow tape, an ambulance with a pair of bored paramedics smoking cigarettes. I'm in the middle of a crime scene again. Why does this keep happening to me?

In a rare show of kindness, Gannon hauls me up and pushes me against the Dumpster with a bone jarring thump. I must look bad because he winces when he's close to me. He backs away, swipes at my blood on his fingers with a handkerchief

"I'll ask again – what are you *doing* here?"

I spin him a story about stopping in for an early morning beer but I can tell he knows it's horseshit. Being partners for five years means Gannon can see through most of my lies. At least the white ones. But that's all he's getting at the moment. The memory of Butch (or was it Dutch?) and his fist still makes me cringe.

Gannon seems unimpressed as I fall into step beside him, just like the old days. There's something comforting in the walking. Like the shit that went down in that Tribeca bar between me and Gray Gary J never happened. Like him stealing my wife never happened. Like we're still partners, still fighting the good fight that Gannon fought so well.

"So you stopped in for a breakfast beer?" my ex-partner asks. "Funny how, out of all the bars in city, you end up here. This being, what, the second dead body I've found you near in less than twelve hours."

Another dead? I light a crumpled Death.

"I have horrible luck," I say.

"Yeah? Not as bad as his though," Gannon says, ushering me into The Closet Skeleton. There, staining the floor like an incomprehensible piece of modern art, are the remains of a man. I say remains, because 90% of his body is ash and only the odd piece of him is left. I say man, because the odd pieces include half a hand, three toes and a dick, all of which are scrabbling across the floor like drunken spiders looking for an easy web. Looks like the Arnie twins had fun.

The CSI guys are hard at work – no sign of Conroy, maybe he's on a date with a necro transvestite. An officer is trying to take the prints of the remaining fingers but the hand keeps trying to break free. I know the feeling.

"The pile of ash is, we believe, one Cyrus Beaumont, the owner," Gannon says. "But why do I think you already know that, Faraday?"

"Who knows where thoughts come from?"

Gannon scowls and I like it.

"How'd he die?"

"Choked on a cheeseball. Jeez, Faraday, has P.I. work made you soft? You need 'em to stand up or you don't know jack shit?"

I throw him a withering glare. "I meant, how did they kill him?"

Now it's Gannon's turn to stare. "*They?* Who said it was more than one killer?"

Shit. I look at the patch that was Cyrus Beaumont, mind working. "A big pile of ash means Cyrus was a big guy," I say. "Would have taken two or more to do him in. One to hold him down, another to...do whatever it is they did."

I remember the undead Arnie's pants leg, the burnt leather of his shoe and the chlorine and gasoline smell. Of course. Let the necro hold him down while the living guy does the killing. Whatever they did would have to be powerful enough to melt brain and bone and leave Cyrus Beaumont with nothing but body shop bits. The chlorine still doesn't make sense but I'm working on it. "Guess I just figured there would be more than one killer," I say.

Gannon seems placated by this, gives me a little for what I just gave him. "You're probably right. *Probably.* But how many killers there were ain't the issue, Faraday. It's what they used."

I kneel. Haven't smelt the sharpness of burnt skin in a while, not since that pyro case from a few years back. Some nut job getting his rocks off setting fire to necro neighbourhoods, tenements in Harlem, warehouses on the Lower East Side, a Church of the Latter Day Dead in Chelsea The stench of those flaming neccers was hideous, the rush of stink that followed when the firemen doused them with foam. Fire doesn't hurt Newly Dead unless it burns hot enough to reduce them to ash – like Cyrus here – but you could tell the neighbourhood necros were scared. The old human responses don't disappear when you die. Dead Americans can still fear death.

But thinking of that pyro makes me wonder how Cyrus bought the fiery farm. On that old case, the pyro had used accelerants based on napalm he'd bought wholesale from Life Supremacists in Utah, but none of his victims had come close to being as damaged as the owner of The Closet Skeleton. From the looks of Cyrus, whatever killed him had burnt fast, and hot. Hell hot.

Gannon reads my mind. "Tough one, huh? Nothing standard could have done this. I got a special investigator from the fire department coming. I told him on the phone what it looked like and he don't believe me. Couldn't even hint at what could do this."

I was waiting for Gannon to say *unknown substance*, the same thing Conroy had called the drug that killed Cherry. A lot of unknown substances floating around New York these days. The lack of answers makes my questions burn like Cyrus had.

Then I take a closer look at the wooden floor. Not only is it blackened – he was definitely burnt, that's true – but the wood's also bubbled, dissolved. I lean as close and sniff. There it is. Chlorine, but stronger then before. It's not really chlorine at all. It just smells like it.

"Acid."

"What?"

I stand, loving the look on Gannon's puffy face. "Acid," I enunciate as if he's a child. "Smells like the pool at the Y, did you notice? Hydrochloric acid smells like chlorine, only sourer, stronger. Given the fire, I'd say they either hit him with acid first, then set him alight, or vice versa. The acid ate his brain, the fire burnt his body.

Probably a cocktail of the shit. Mix it all together and throw in a lit match." Gannon's eyeing me warily. "Just a guess."

"And how do you know all this?" he asks.

"I read. C'mon, don't look at me like that, Ray. You can buy the stuff anywhere. Hell, go to the nearest high school and you'll find some in the science lab. In fact, you should check to see if any schools have reported stolen hydrochloric acid. I don't think the guys that did this are as smart as you think."

Gannon has hate in his eyes and that's my cue to leave. "Well, good luck," I say. "Looks like you're in for a long day."

My former partner gives me a, "Hmph," and opens his notebook. "You ain't getting off that easy, Faraday. How did you know the deceased?"

"I didn't."

"Horseshit."

"Never met him before."

"Then why was your card in what remains of his pocket?"

It's my turn to grunt. Oh, well. Truth time. "I came here last night following a lead. I thought Cherry Hampton may have been a regular. I ran into a little trouble with some z-boys, left my card with a barmaid, and I was coming back to see the owner – Cyrus you say? – when I was mugged. End of story."

Gannon's chewing a toothpick. He thinks it makes him look tough, and he's right. "That's it, huh? Who were these z-boys?"

"Charlie and Linus."

"Where was Snoopy?"

"Fuck you."

"Were they the ones who mugged you?"

"No."

"Who was it?"

I smoke. I don't want to tell Gannon about the Arnie twins.

They are obviously prime suspects in Cyrus' spontaneous combustion but Gannon doesn't know that. And I like it when I know more than him.

Eventually I say, "Couldn't tell. It was dark."

"At eight o'clock in the morning?"

I shrug. I'm not going to give him the satisfaction of responding and he looks like he's had enough.

"*Do yourself a favour*, Faraday." Here we go. "Get the fuck out of my crime scene."

I shrug again, heading for the door. There's nothing for me here. Cyrus isn't exactly in the position to answer any of my questions, and I can't really show Cherry's photo to his big toe. If I spent any more time around Gannon I'd be tempted to ask about Brenda, and I don't want to.

As Gannon grumbles at his team, using that brusque way of his to get things moving, my thoughts are on Dutch and Butch. Hard motherfuckers. Burn a man to death with acid so he can't relive. But why leave the fingers, the toes, the penis? They must have had a reason. Probably so the cops could identify Cyrus. But why? So the cops would have a lead. Why? The bar must be a front for his side business with Grandpa Hob, Cyrus must have been into something more than just pulling beers for the dead. But what? Ready Ronnie Sikes had said Cyrus ran girls but why would Butch and Dutch toast him for that?

Unknown. Like those unknown substances you keep hearing about.

A young forensic tech is having trouble with what's left of Cyrus' penis. The cock has wedged itself under the bathroom door, though God only knows what it was doing heading that way. Probably instinctual. I know how the dick feels.

Chapter 8
The Girl Hunters

My Chevy is in park but my thoughts are driving. Cherry Hampton. Sorority girl turned runaway. Dead. Really dead. Overdosed on a drug with no name. What? Cyrus Beaumont. Owner of The Closet Skeleton. Ash. Zombie penis. Burnt up by acid. Why? The twins. Butch and Dutch. One dead, one living. Raybans and CIA radios. Who's on the other end of the line? Fists the size of planets. Annoying diction. Definitely toasted Cyrus. What for? Gannon. Asshole. One step behind me, every which way I turn. Asshole. One armed Charlie and Linus. Why am I even thinking of them? Dorothy the barmaid. Dorothy. Dorothy. There'd been something about what Dorothy had said...

Is she...dead? Dorothy had asked last night, a tremor in her voice. I thought at the time she was shocked just to see a dead person, thought she was surprised Cherry wasn't undead. But what if Dorothy had been lying? What if Dorothy really did know Cherry and hadn't wanted to tell me? Why would Dorothy be contrary?

Ten minutes later there's a newspaper on my lap and I'm sitting in my Chevy a quarter block down from The Closet Skeleton. The ambulance has moved on, Gannon's nowhere to be seen and a lone patrolman is keeping guard at the entrance as the last of the forensics guys leave. Soon the uniform will lock the door, lash it

61

with yellow tape and head for a doughnut.

I drum the steering wheel. I call Hampton, get the machine, apologize for being a little late (the appointment was an hour ago), and say I'll be there as soon as possible.

Drumming the steering wheel some more does little for my patience. Never been good with waiting. Stakeouts shit me. Action is the enemy of thought, and when there's more thought than action, that can be just as bad .

My last day as a detective. The back room of that fucking bar in Tribeca. A girl not much older than Cherry Hampton. A girl with stringy blonde hair, a face ravaged by junk and AIDS and tricks. Gray Gary J and his shit eating grin. Fire. Fire, everywhere.

A taxi horn snaps me back and there's Dorothy the barmaid coming up the street wrapped in a red jacket. I can see her rosy cheeks from here.

She stops when she sees the yellow taped door. She seems surprised, shocked. She looks around and I shrink back into the car seat and lift up the newspaper from my lap. Just a guy reading a paper in his car, Dorothy, not suspicious at all. But I needn't have worried, as Dorothy's already walking away, quickly. A little too fast, my cop instinct tells me.

I ditch the Chevy and thread through the traffic on foot. Dorothy's got a head start but that red jacket is a dead giveaway. She's heading for Sheridan Square, cutting through the press of trendy dead bohemians the Village attracts. She skips down the steps to the Christopher Street subway station. Great. I hate riding the subway. Like a big, fast moving coffin. But I have to talk to Dorothy. The questions itch at me.

My footsteps are swallowed by the combined noise of the trains rattling by and the dozens of other commuters. It's cool down here and it's no wonder the subway stations attract the Newly Dead. Earthen, underground, away from the light – like a crypt they can walk around in.

I shoulder through a group of necro schoolchildren, on some sightseeing trip by the look. Must suck being dead and still having to go to school. Would really make you wonder at the point of algebra.

Dorothy's heading for the uptown local, one of the central cars. She slips out of sight when I'm jostled by a Dead Chinese woman whose chunky suitcase looks like it has her dead husband inside. The necro hisses something at me and I don't need to be a linguist to guess what. I help lift her bag on the train – definitely heavy enough to house a corpse – and she curses at me in Mandarin as she waddles off down the aisle. Nice. Used to be the dead didn't give attitude. I long for the old days.

The train starts off as I inch towards Dorothy's car. Rush hour is 9 to 5 in New York and the commuters are thick. The fact I'm hurtling like a bullet through a tunnel doesn't help my social skills and I bump elbows, disturb newspapers.

"Asshole," a little old lady mutters, and some mook (or should that be Dead Irish American?) says, "I'm standing here!" but I'm too busy to retort. Dorothy's in the next car along.

By the time I reach the interconnecting door, the train is slowing for the 14th Street Station and Dorothy hasn't seen me yet. She's biting her lip, staring into space, and her fingers nervously tap the umbrella she's holding. Scared. What does she know that makes her tremble so?

The train stops with a shush. I step into her carriage but the outer doors swish open and a vomit of people, dead and living, spew into the aisle. For a second Dorothy's lost in the press of bodies, until I step on an armrest and hoist myself up with a handle. There she is.

Wait. Who's she looking at?

I follow Dorothy's gaze and see the reason she looks more scared than before. A pair of necros have gotten on the train, one with a buzz cut around a head wound, the other with a metal brace keeping his head on straight. Charlie and Linus. My two favourite z-boys.

The necro toughs don't have my flair for politeness – they're pushing people out of the way, eyes only for Dorothy. Linus is giggling but Charlie is stone quiet, nothing like he was last night. He shoves an obese necro aside like she weighs less than Paris Hilton's corpse and he's got his arm back, laser spliced to the wound I made and good as new. Better. The new arm is blacker than the rest of him and looks almost comical sticking from Charlie's ripped denim jacket. But the arm's corded with muscle, powerful – not funny in the slightest really. That arm looks like it could choke a joke to death.

I push forward but I'm too late. Dorothy turns and sees the z-boys right in front of her.

It takes a second for the shock to wear off and then Dorothy's running, or at least trying to run in the packed carriage. But she isn't quick enough – Charlie grabs her wrist, wrenches her to him and whips his new arm around her throat. She manages a scream that shocks the passengers to silence.

The crowd in the train surges, a woman cries out and I'm held back. I draw my Beretta, hoping the sight of the gun might clear the way, but there's nothing in my holster. Remember, Faraday? The Arnie twins took it when they kicked your ass.

Shit.

Charlie has his dead face against Dorothy's rosy cheek, whispering into her hair. He's dragging her backwards, the commuters shrinking from him. Linus is dancing around waving a switchblade knife like it's Excalibur.

I break free of the crowd and yell, "Hey!"

Linus drops the switchblade with a yelp. *What a tool.* "Ch, Ch, Charlie – it's, it's the guy from the bar!"

His metal brace bobs as he runs his hand over his forearm in a sawing motion. "M, member? The, the one who c, c, c-"

"Shut up," Charlie hisses. He flexes and Dorothy moans. He's choking her and her cheeks aren't so rosy anymore.

"Whatcha want, huh, Mr Heroman? Nothing for you here."

Linus scrabbles the knife back into his hand and crouches low. He looks like he's going to jump out of his skin. But Charlie – Charlie's cold. Charlie's clear. Charlie's in charge. So I play it.

"Dorothy there must be pretty important for Grandpa Hob to send you boys after her," I say. "This wouldn't have anything to do with a girl named Cherry now, would it?" I lean against a seat, trying to act casual. Charlie ain't buying what I'm selling. Nothing's changed. The z-boy's inscrutable.

Linus' ragged mouth makes an O. "How, how, how," he gapes.

"I said shut up!" Charlie hollers, the façade cracking. "Fuck you, Linus, you deadshit. Now git the goddamn door!"

"B, b, b..."

"Git the door! You! Heroman! You git back now or I'll do her, I will."

I throw out a hook: "Like you did Cherry?"

"Git back!" he says, not biting.

The train rocks on its tracks, darkness speeding by the windows. Dorothy's turning blue, he's killing her anyway, but he could break her neck before I reach him. It's a no-win situation anyway you look at it.

Linus has his knife in the door, prying it open, and suddenly the stale air of the carriage is buffeted with diesel stink wind. The crowd is swept back fearfully. Someone hits the emergency button and the conductor hits the brakes. We all lurch.

"We gitting off this train," Charlie says, "me and Linus and her. And you better stay where you are."

"What are you going to do?" I ask. The train's slowing.

Charlie gives me a lecherous grin. Then he runs his grey tongue up Dorothy's cheek, drooling. "Whatcha think, huh?"

Dorothy's brown eyes plead with me. If he kills her, I'll never forget that look.

"Out, Linus!" Charlie says, putting a boot to the other z-boy's back. Linus flails out the open carriage door and Charlie throws himself after him. They land in a puff of dust and unfortunately there isn't another train coming the right way to take care of them for me. Great. I hate subway tunnels.

I rush to the window in time to see Charlie skidding in the pebbly soil between the tracks, Dorothy held to his chest. Sonofabitch. No pain means necros can do things the living can't. Like jump from moving trains.

The train is still going too fast – if I jump now a lot of bones would break and I'm quite attached to them – and I wait, I wait, I wait until I can't wait any more before I throw myself out the door and into underground air. The second before the ground rushes up to meet me I wonder if I should have checked to see if a train was coming this time.

Then my left shoulder hits scathing ground and there's a pop and my shoulder flares as I roll and roll and stop.

My shoulder feels dislocated, a red tinged numbness too sharp to be held back by the adrenaline. Shadows are moving up the tunnel, one holding a struggling second, a third shadow with metal struts sticking from its back tagging along. I push myself into a hobbling run, holding my left arm tight against my side. The pain's good. Pain means I'm still alive.

The z-boys cut into a side passage, some type of maintenance shaft by the look. Why did they do that? I can see the lights of the station up ahead, it isn't far – why didn't they head for the station?

Then I realise the light isn't a station. It's an oncoming train.

I throw my back against the wall as tons of rocketing metal screeches an inch from my face. The motion makes my heels rock, centrifugal force pulls me forward. I tense, jab my fingers between the bricks at my back. Fingernails break, warm blood flows. My skin ripples, my jacket snapping like a flag.

Then it's over, the train a blur speeding away. I slump against the track.

But a moment later I'm up, following the echo of Linus' giggle down the maintenance tunnel.

It's dark. Up ahead there's blue light.

"Do, do you think it got him?" Linus asks.

"Yeh, now c'mon. We got to git this done."

My shoulder's an ache without end and I slow my steps, slow my breathing. The tunnel widens into a long room, benches set in the middle. Some type of locker room for tunnel workers.

The necro scumbags and their pretty piece are just ahead of me, near a set of lockers lit by a blue bulb set in the ceiling. I shrink into some convenient shadows, inch closer.

Dorothy's lying on one of the wooden benches, unmoving. It looks like they've killed her until I see her chest still rising and falling. Unconscious. Charlie probably choked her until she passed out.

Linus is behind Dorothy's head, holding open a hessian bag. Charlie is standing over her, drawing something long and wicked from his denim jacket. A machete, glinting devilishly in the weird blue light.

"I like, like, like this part," Linus says.

Charlie grins at him.

The necro hefts the blade and brings it swinging down on Dorothy's neck. In the instant before the machete slices flesh, the girl's eyes flicker open and her sharp intake of breath is like a death rattle, the last breath she'll ever take.

"NO DON'T CUT ME DON'T CUT ME!" Dorothy cries for her life.

I scream out but it's too late.

There's a clunk as the blade sinks into the bench and Dorothy's severed head rolls into Linus' bag. Blood jets from the stump of Dorothy's neck, staining the hessian bag.

The z-boys look up in surprise. Linus points down the corridor, finger waggling like a dying fish. "He ain't d, d, dead Charlie!" Linus whimpers.

"Git him!"

Linus giggles again – I hate that fucking giggle – and slinks towards me, his switchblade flashing. Charlie picks up the bag with Dorothy's head and wipes the machete off. For an instant I stand my ground. Then there's the realisation that I'm fighting two armed necros with nothing but my fists and a dislocated shoulder. It would be like punching a wall that never stopped punching back. I need a plan.

I turn and run.

Linus' metal brace clicks like a wild maraca player as he chases me, Charlie's evil laugh dogging my heels.

"Catch 'im, Linus," Charlie calls, "catch 'im and we'll have two heads to take to Grandpa!"

I burst from the tunnel onto the train tracks. They're blessedly clear and the station must be close. But something hard hits me, Linus jumping on my back, and forces me to the ground.

The air is knocked from my lungs. There are stars

in my eyes instead of birds this time, and Linus is chattering like a monkey, "I got him, got him, got him!"

The thought of Charlie's machete is too much and I jam my elbow into Linus sunken rib cage and heave. He's a bag of bones and steel and it's easy to flip him over so I'm on top of him. A foot on his wrist and the switchblade knife is mine. His milky white eyes are wide and if necros could still piss their pants I'd be smelling his by now. He stinks bad enough without it.

"D, d, d, d," he stutters as I pick him up by his collar and stand. My shoulder is nothing but pain yet it's totally worth it to see the look on Linus' face. His teeth are crooked, spindly, like the broken picket fence of a haunted house. Necros aren't known for their hygiene.

"What, Linus?"

"D, d, d, d..."

"Dead, Linus?" I ask as I shove him backwards.

He totters for a step and falls. His metal braces strike the tracks and sparks fly. Linus has connected the tracks with the steel frame in his back and he jolts as a couple of thousand volts of electricity slams through his dead body. He's on the ground dancing and jumping and screaming but it's a muted sound because he can't seem to form words. Ozone fills the air, as well as burning flesh as Linus catches fire.

I think of Gray Gary J.

Linus' jittering finally breaks the connection between the tracks. His smoking corpse slumps in the dirt. His skin is black as tar, the metal brace scorched, and he isn't moving. Electrocution doesn't kill Newly Dead. But it's bought me some time at least.

From the maintenance tunnel: "Linus! Where are ya, deadshit?"

Charlie's close so I hobble over to the tunnel, crouch beside the entrance. Everything's going blurry around the edges as my adrenaline fast runs out. If I faint now I'm dead, and Charlie doesn't look the type to let me relive peacefully. After what I just did to his buddy, I'll be ash for Ole Hob's fireplace.

I clutch the switchblade, such a pathetic weapon against necros, as Charlie's footsteps boom from the tunnel. He must be dragging the bag – there's a swishing sound as well – and as he clears the tunnel I tense against the wall.

The z-boy's looking at the remains of his friend and he hardens, become more alert. His new black arm holds the bag with Dorothy's head, the machete in the other.

Now.

I leap up and slam the switchblade into his nice, new arm. The glint of surprise in his eyes is pure gold. The force behind my attack makes the knife go through his forearm and into the wall and the shock's enough to make him drop the bag. He's caught.

Charlie howls but he's not as dim as Linus, and he brings the machete around, hacking at me. I duck the blow, scoop up the bag, and jump down onto the tracks.

"Fucker!" Charlie hollers after me. "I'll git you, Heroman! You're mine!"

He's probably right. The knife was never going to hold him for long. There's a sickening rend as Charlie pulls his arm through the switchblade – fucking neccers, is there nothing they can't do? – and his laughter cuts me more than his machete could. "That the best ya got?"

I try to think of something clever to say but nothing comes to mind. Running away will have do to as a retort.

The bag with Dorothy's head is heavy, bouncing against my thigh with every step, almost tripping me up on the tracks. But there's light ahead and I hobble towards it, hoping for salvation.

"I'm talking to you, Heroman!" Charlie hollers.

I glance over my shoulder and he's striding behind

me, obviously savouring the fact that all I can do is limp away from him. He'll be on me in a matter of seconds.

"You want me...come and get me!" I know what you're thinking. Not the best line but, like I said before, wit is the furthest thing from my mind.

The light at the end of the tunnel is rushing closer and it's time to press my luck again. I throw the bag with Dorothy's head to the side and put up my dukes. Well, one of my dukes since I can't lift the other one because of my shoulder. I must look as pathetic as I feel.

"You should have kept out of Grandpa Hob's business," the necro smirks as he comes closer. He flexes his black arm and the wound from my knife attack is a dark hole. It looks like he could wrestle God with that arm. Or the Devil at least. "Now you gonna die and I'm gonna make you my bitch!"

"Tempting,"

Wind is buffeting my hair, the ground is vibrating and that light behind me is coming up fast, faster than a speeding bullet. Over my shoulder the light is so bright, so close.

Charlie must have finally realised what's happening, as he stops, the machete going limp in his hand. His puzzled frown is just about the sweetest thing I've ever seen.

"Give my regards to Grandpa!" I cry, throwing my body to the side and hitting the wall with a bone jarring thump. A shiver of pain burns my shoulder but that's nothing compared to what's about to happen to Charlie.

He's still stunned – those z-boys, so confident, so ignorant – and all he can do is whimper as the A train slams into him like a fast-moving mountain.

For an instant I can make out the startled look on the subway driver's fat face – a Dead African American by the look, they always give jobs like that to necros – and then the tunnel is filled with the screeching of the brakes, sparks flying, the wind of its passage making a maelstrom of the dust. But it's too late for Charlie.

The A train makes a brown smear out of the z-boy and it's satisfying to see bits of Charlie fly off – his shiny new arm, a leg, part of his torso. His nose even bounces off the wall near my head and lands at my feet. I stomp on it. And it feels good.

The train is grinding to a stop. I've got to get out of here – I like my own questions, not the ones I'd get for this fiasco – and I scoop up the bag with Dorothy's head and make for the blue lit tunnel. The maintenance tunnel should lead outside. At least I hope so, because right now I can't wait to see the sun.

Dorothy's head bag is a lump in my hand. The bag leaves a bloody smear on my pants with every step up the tunnel. Dorothy's headless corpse is lying on the metal bench and a pang of regret hits me like *deja vu*. Couldn't save you, Dorothy.

But at least I have her head. At least I can still get some answers to my questions.

Chapter 9
The Body Lovers

By the time sunlight hits me I'm in Chelsea, hobbling up 8th Avenue and trying not to notice the look I'm getting from the openly gay mixed life couple on the corner of 17th Street. Their matching spandex jogging suits are ludicrous – pink and green and black, if you can believe it – but I can't laugh because I really don't have the time.

The bag with Dorothy's head is a sodden weight and I'm thankful the head hasn't relived yet, but the jogging partners are staring at me, then the bag, then at me. I sneak a peek at my reflection in the window of a diner. I look as bad as Dorothy, my jacket torn from my tussle with Linus, blood smearing my pants, my face a ghostly black from the grit of the subway. Probably look worse than any necro the joggers have ever seen.

I don't know where I'm going – I have a vague notion to head back to my office but there's no way I'm taking the subway again this century and the thought of walking the dozen or so blocks with a decapitated head in my hand is as depressing as it sounds. Besides, it would be just my luck that Dorothy will relive before I reach the East Village and I don't know what would be worse – the questions she'd ask or the ones I'd get from passers-by when they see me talking to a corpseless head.

My dislocated shoulder is a demon. It feels like it's dragging me down with every step, like I'm lumbering under some mammoth weight, and I need to see someone, anyone. Doctor, nurse, veterinarian, hell I'd settle for a homeless guy with a Band-Aid right about now. I'd even settle for Conroy.

There's a thought. The forensic pathologist would not only have access to some great drugs –the delicious thought of a painkiller makes me shiver – but he'd also help me with the head. Probably want to keep her afterwards too, knowing him.

Figuring any plan is better than no plan, I hail an oncoming cab and it screeches to a stop in front of me. The driver's a Newly Dead and I figure he stopped because he thought I was the same. Reverse lifism is everywhere in New York.

"Geez, what happened to you?" the driver asks with awe in his voice. He's missing his nose, it looks like a crow's had a go at his left eye, and by his girth he looks like a heart attack that's already happened.

I toss him a soiled twenty, mumble, "Police Plaza," resist the urge to say, "and step on it," and settle back.

The twenty's the best answer I could have given and he pulls out into the traffic, cutting off a bicycle courier and a bus at the same time. New York taxis. If there's a machine that's more like a New Yorker than a cab, I've yet to see it.

I cradle Dorothy's head in my lap. I'm beyond caring if blood gets on me anymore.

"Where ya been to get like that?" the necro asks, arching an eyebrow in the rear view.

"Subway."

"Ah." Cabbies. They either know everything or make out they do. Then he adds: "What's in the bag?"

"Laundry day."

"Ah."

I can feel a conversation coming on so I pull out my phone and dial Conroy's office. It rings twice before a nasally voice says, "Forensics."

I ask for Conroy, get a nasally reply, and after five seconds of dead air I hear, "This is Francis Conroy."

"Francis? I worked with you for five years and I never knew your name was Francis."

A beat. "Faraday. I don't know whether to hang up or say fuck you."

"Usually people do the latter before the former, but I find it works either way." Conroy must be pissed about the necro transvestite. I can imagine the look on his ratty face. Shame. Who would have thought he and Lady Macabre wouldn't have hit it off?

"What do you want?"

The necro cabbie is eyeing me in the rear view – well, at least his right eye is, the left's just hanging there – and I hold the phone tighter, lower my voice. I hate eavesdropping unless I'm the one doing it. I tell Conroy I have something interesting for him.

Conroy barks a laugh. "What? A necro *hermaphrodite* this time?"

He's pissed but I talk him down, manage to get him to meet me at the back carpark of Police Plaza by convincing him I had nothing to do with the phone number mix up – "Must have been Heidi, slipping you a mickey."

"Humph," Conroy grunts. "All right, Faraday. I'll be there."

"Great," I say, relieved. Then, I can't help myself, and add: "See you soon...Francis."

I close the phone on Conroy's "fuck you".

The streets roll by and soon the monolithic home of New York's finest is outside my window.

"Have a nice d-" the cabbie tries to say but I slam the door on such an optimistic goodbye. Not in the mood today.

There's an undercover cop coming down the stairs – you can always tell them by the way they walk – and his eyes narrow when he sees my shabby condition, my stumbling gait, the blood stained hessian bag clutched in my hand. I give him a tired nod that says, *Tough day on the beat,* and it works. I must look more like a cop then I feel.

Conroy's waiting for me right where he said, coughing after every puff of a cigarette. What a tool. Must have bummed the smoke to cover leaving his office. I learnt long ago that confidence is the best cover.

"What's that?" Conroy points the smouldering end of his smoke at the bag.

"This is Dorothy," I say, grabbing the cigarette from his hand. I take a puff. Gah. Menthol.

"Dorothy? Your bag's named Dorothy?" Conroy's looking at me as if I'm crazy. But his smug smile falters when I open the bag and he sees the bloody head inside.

"Jesus."

"Right. Shall we?" I ask, tipping my chin towards the Plaza.

Ten minutes later I'm shrugging off my torn jacket and blood-stained shirt and hoping forensic pathologists know a thing or two about treating live people. We're in one of the old autopsy rooms, long disused since the dead came back to life. A layer of dust covers the floor and the equipment has been stacked in one corner haphazardly. It's almost forlorn until Conroy makes a hell of a racket dragging a steel table away from the wall.

He sees me wince at the sound and grins. "Don't worry, Faraday. The noise doesn't matter. Nobody comes down here anymore."

"I can see why."

He shrugs, almost sadly. "This used to be my favourite room," he says, looking around. "Now I'm lucky if I even get to leave my desk. It's no fun being a pathologist any more."

Conroy jabs me with a needle – "A cocktail, to help with the pain," he calls it – and as a lovely warmth spreads through my body, he gently probes my dislocated shoulder.

"How'd you do this?"

"The A train. Rush hour's a bitch."

Conroy grunts. "Okay. This is going to hurt."

It does. Conroy enjoys popping my shoulder back into place a little too much but I can't complain because I'm trying not to bite my tongue off. His cocktail of painkillers deadens the residual pain though, and soon all that's left is a dull ache.

"Better? Good. Now – let me have a look at this head."

Without waiting for a reply, Conroy overturns the bag and Dorothy's head rolls onto the table. He picks her up, turns her in his hands, says, "Hmm." He lays her on her cheek beside me. I don't like being this close to the head so I get off the table, staggering slightly. Conroy's painkillers are working overtime.

"I'd say cause of death is decapitation," Conroy muses.

"You think?"

He continues like I'm not even there. "The cut was definitely not post mortem – see the arteries here, and here, empty of blood, probably bled out the instant she was cut. I'd say...a long instrument. Some sort of knife, or even a sword by the looks."

"How about a machete?"

"Ah, yes, makes sense. No serrated edges. Hmm. Yes. Very, very interesting. Shame you didn't bring the rest of her with you. That would make it easier to establish time of death."

"No need," I say. Picturing Dorothy's headless body back in the subway tunnel is not something to reminisce about, so I hastily add, "She died about fifteen, twenty minutes ago."

"Hmm. Shouldn't be too long until she relives then. Unless..."

He wants to mention Cherry Hampton, but doesn't. It's been so long since there was any doubt about what happens when you die. Conroy doesn't know what to think. There'll be a lot of people in New York, in America, feeling the same way today.

The world's going blurry around the edges and sleep feels good at the moment, too good. But if I fell asleep now my questions wouldn't be answered and I hate having unanswered questions. Besides, God only knows what Conroy would do with a Newly Dead head when no one's around. I shudder to think.

"Uh oh," Conroy says. "Someone's coming."

He sounds like he's just being paranoid – Conroy always been the nervous type – but I follow his frantic pointing with my eyes and sure enough he's right. Through the mottled window of the door there are two figures coming down the hall towards the autopsy room.

"Quick! Get in!"

Conroy's opened one of the meat lockers and slid out the table. They used to keep dead bodies in these between autopsies. It looks dark and too closed in for my tastes.

"No way," I say. "Tell them I'm an intern."

Conroy's eyes are bugging. "Faraday, get in!" he hisses. "If anyone finds you here it will cost me my job. With your rep, I could end up sharing your jail cell!"

The locker is a gaping black hole. I hate gaping black holes. "Can't I just...?"

"No time," and even as he says it I know he's right. The heavy steps of one of the people are getting closer, the other's high heels click-click-clicking in counterpoint. They're too close.

I sit on the table, slide around to lie down, and I

huff as Conroy throws Dorothy's head on my lap. "Hey!"
I cry but Conroy's not listening, he's already pushing the
slide-out table back into the locker.

The darkness crowds my feet, my thighs, my chest,
my face. Claustrophobia claws at my heart and
instinctively I grip Dorothy's head, as if she can offer me
some comfort. But all I get is more blood on me.

"Don't make a sound," Conroy whispers, slamming
the door shut and plunging me into pure black.

Instantly tense. I've never been good with confined
spaces. But there's nothing to do except wait. At least I
can hear what's going on outside.

The door opens with a rusty scrape.

"Ah, hello there, Detective *Gannon*," Conroy pipes.
I'm guessing he made a point of the surname for me.
"And...guest. Hello."

I can imagine Gannon's unflinching glare. "What
are you doing down here?"

A rustling sound, as if Conroy's picked up the
bloodied bag. "Overtime," Conroy sighs, a little too
dramatically. "Just came down to get a closer look at this.
An old case, new evidence."

"Looks fresh," Gannon grunts.

Stupid, Conroy. A detective knows the difference
between new blood and old blood. But Conroy covers well:
"That's what I told them but I'm not paid to ask questions,
apparently. What do I know, huh?"

Obviously Gannon buys it, for his answering grunt
is almost sympathetic. There's another rustling, this time
of paper. "Take a look at this. Results of that guy who
was burnt up in Greenwich this morning."

Ah. Cyrus Beaumont. I resist the urge to scrunch
closer to the door to hear better. Probably make too much
noise. Dorothy's head is like a slab of meat on my
stomach. Cold and dead.

Conroy flips page after page. "Hmm...traces of

gasoline ...strong dose of HCl, hydrochloric acid....hmm. Interesting. Acid and oil. It's no wonder there wasn't much left of him. The acid would have eaten through the brain while the fire burnt up the rest of him. At these doses, it's like a science experiment gone wrong."

Gannon rips the file from Conroy's hands. "Fucking Faraday."

"What do you mean?" another voice, a woman asks.

My heart skips.

I know that voice.

"Nothing," my ex-partner says.

The woman taps a Prada on the floor the way she always does when she's irritated. It's a hollow sound. "Nothing? Well, that's exactly what you have against my client, *Detective* Gannon. I can't believe you brought *him* in – and *me* down here – for this."

Gannon must be chewing another one of those goddamn toothpicks 'cause something snaps. Then again it might be his nerves. "Your client was brought in for routine questioning..."

"There's nothing routine about this, Ray. Now, unless you have some evidence that links my client to this Cyrus Beaumont, I suggest you-"

Picking exactly the wrong moment to relive, the dead head on my lap jerks and splutters and screams, "NO DON'T CUT ME DON'T CUT ME!" The force of Dorothy's reliving makes it feel as if she's going to jump out of my hands (somehow), hit the wall of the locker and give me away.

But my instincts are quicker then I give them credit for because jam my hand over her mouth tight and I pray and I wait and I pray. I've seen this sort of thing before, when a fresh Newly Dead reacts to the event that killed her. It's like replay on a DVD. Dorothy still thinks she's back in the subway and her yelling is a feeble attempt to stop Charlie's falling machete.

"What the fuck was that?" Gannon brusquely asks and his heavy shoes take a step towards my hiding spot. Dorothy's struggling against my grip, nipping at my fingers. I put my other hand over my own mouth because the bitch has sharp teeth.

Conroy sounds nervous when he says, "What? I didn't hear anything."

The blood means my hand's slippery and somehow Dorothy's wriggled free, and she yells again, "NO DON'T CUT ME DON'T CUT ME!!" before I can shut her up.

"There it is again," Gannon says, clearly suspicious. "Did you hear it?"

"Ah, um, yes..." Conroy stutters. He walks towards the meat lockers – the mother's going to give me away to save his own skin! – but right before the door he stops, scrounges around and there's an electronic click.

"It's just, um, my mobile, the, ahem, ring tone."

"Your ring tone is a girl screaming for help?" the woman with Gannon asks incredulously.

"Um, yeah. From, um, *Dawn of the Dead.* I, ah...sampled it myself."

There's a beat.

Dorothy finally stops struggling.

I'm breathing way too loud.

But Conroy's gambit works.

"You're sick, Conroy," Gannon says, his footsteps moving away from the meat locker. "One. Sick. Fuck."

The door opens, the hinges squeaking, and then the click-click of high heels and Gannon's own meaty footsteps recede up the hall.

I keep my hand clamped to Dorothy's mouth until I hear the snap of the locker door. Conroy slides the table out, making me blink in the sudden brightness. I look down and Dorothy's milky, dead eyes stare back at me. She's obviously surprised to see me.

"Are you going to keep quiet?" I ask Dorothy and

something in my tone makes her relax (as much as a severed head can relax at all). "I'm going to take my hand away, okay?" I wait for her to nod and almost laugh at how stupid I can be sometimes. "Wink if you understand."

She blinks and somehow makes the motion seem haughty. There's that dead attitude again. Great.

I sit up, hold Dorothy gently by her hair, and put her on the table beside me. She doesn't say anything. Probably still in shock. Death can do that to you.

Conroy's smiling nervously, grinning really. "Phew, that was close. Good thing I thought of my phone, huh? That Gannon can be a real hard ass. And that woman he had with him – the power suit, the smirk. She seemed like a real ball breaker."

"She is."

Conroy frowns. "You know her?"

"Yeah." I don't want to say it but I have to. "That was Brenda Barrett. My ex-wife."

Chapter 10
The King in Yellow

Brenda Barrett. Brenda, Brenda Barrett. Brenda, Brenda, Brenda. The whole thing was wrong from the start but that's hindsight and I rarely look back with rose coloured glasses.

It's the same old story. She, a young district attorney coming up through the ranks. Me, a detective helping her put the scum behind bars. Brenda once told me it was my attitude she liked most, the fact I didn't give a shit what people thought of me. I liked the way she smiled. And the sex.

We were married a week after she went pro, gave up the DA office and started defending the scumbags. Don't get me wrong, she made a lot of money doing it and used to joke that she was my sugar mama. But with every day that passed, every bad guy she defended and got out – and it was a few, she's good at her job – I started to realise the vicious circle we were in. I'd put them away, she'd set them free. We started fighting at night, then in the morning. The sex dropped off after that. So did the smiles.

Gray Gary J was really the last straw.

I'm thinking about him, and her, while walking down the steps of Police Plaza. Dorothy's in an *I loveheart NY* bag that Conroy generously donated. I swear he was salivating as he helped me put Dorothy's head in the bag.

Dirty. Actually asked if I could leave Dorothy with him, so he could *run a few tests* as he put it. Yeah, right. I know exactly what tests he meant.

I'm also wearing a new shirt, something ludicrous that Conroy fetched from his office, a pink and yellow Hawaiian affair that looks like it was thrown up by Jackson Pollack's corpse. Conroy's little version of a joke, but when your shirt's covered with blood and ripped from a subway tussle with a couple of z-boys, can you really complain? Luckily the shirt is loud enough to stop people looking at my face and I make it to the steps out front without being noticed. But what's happening on the pavement stops me from walking on.

There's Brenda, surrounded by a mob of reporters and cameras and microphones. I have to admit she looks good. Bitch. Standing beside her is someone I didn't expect to see. Or someone I could have happily gone my whole life and half of my afterlife without ever meeting again. Brenda's most valuable client.

Grandpa Hob.

He's flanked by a couple of his z-boys, probably the most respectable looking of his undead toughs given their white bread looks. He's a small man, Hob, smaller than you'd think. To me he always looks like a shriveled Santa Claus. All bones and beard and dirty, lost dreams. The dead kingpin of Harlem, who could pass as just another wizened old skeleton playing chess in Central Park with all the other walking corpses. But if you knew Hob, you'd know that appearances aren't everything.

The first time I met him he was still alive. Caught on a routine traffic violation – busted taillight – and found with a pound of formalin coke in the trunk of his car. Never went to court, of course. Why would he? He has Brenda Barrett as his lawyer supreme, so why should he do time for any crime he commits? Fucking Harvard law school has a lot to answer for.

Today he's wearing a rather nice Armani – the dead still have taste – and he can't smell that bad because Brenda is right up against him, hand on his shoulder. Then again, she is a lawyer, so she's paid enough to stand the smell of rotting flesh for at least a little while. She does sleep with Gannon, which is quite similar. Or so I hear.

"My client has been falsely accused and harassed by the NYPD," my ex-wife is saying. She's said the same thing a million times and not once has it been remotely true. "My client will be seeking damages, should the police continue with this blatant harassment of such a decent, upstanding member of society."

Only a few of the reporters smirk at this and it's no wonder. Even a jerk like me would find it hard to joke about Grandpa Hob. At least to his dead face. Ole Hob looks like he's having a great time. That grin of his would give a nun a heart attack.

Brenda's still on her soapbox: "My client is well known in Harlem for his community outreach work with both the living and the Newly Dead, and the NYPD would do well to realise the damage that malicious and unsubstantiated allegations such as this can do."

I'm slipping past the mob – the Hawaiian shirt, amazingly, acts almost like camouflage (I imagine people think I'm just some slob because of the colour and cut) – when I notice a certain reporter on the edge of the pack. The suit. The smirk. The microphone. Kastle with a K.

"Ms Barrett, how do you respond to allegations that your client is one of the city's biggest dealers in methamphetamines? Prostitution, racketeering? Murder?"

Subtle. Evidently Kastle doesn't mind going for Hob's throat in front of him. The dead chick's got balls.

Brenda swats Kastle's questions aside as if they're flies. "As I *said*, this is all part of the ongoing harassment of my client by the NYPD, and should more of these malicious *allegations* continue to surface – especially on *your* network, Ms Kastle – rest assured it is not only the police we will be seeking damages from."

Smooth riposte from Brenda, I like it. Says so much without really saying anything. Nice spin.

But Alison Kastle with a K cannot be outdone. "Okay. How about this – how do you respond to allegations your client is involved with the Omega America scandal?"

Boom. I think it was Spider Jerusalem who said journalism is a shotgun. Aim it right and you can kneecap the world. Well, Kastle has good aim. The pack of reporters must like it too, judging by how many ask the same question but in different ways.

Brenda takes the cue and begins to press through the microphones. "There will be no further comment," she says and they only part a little, but when Grandpa Hob's toughs push, the reporters reluctantly pull back.

"No comment then, Ms Barrett?" Alison Kastle says, but she's not really asking. She's just happy she got the reaction on camera.

There's a black Lincoln idling at the curb and the driver's eyeing me warily because I just happen to be walking down the steps parallel to Grandpa. But before I cut away – I want to go somewhere quiet to have a stiff drink before I talk to the stiff's head – Grandpa Hob stops at the car door.

Ole Hob sees me. Raises a shriveled eyebrow. Oh yeah. He remembers me.

"Who is it...?" I hear Brenda ask, but I'm already walking away, hunching my shoulders further into my Hawaiian shirt, hoping she doesn't realise who caught her mobster boss' attention. Talking with one dead head is more than enough for me today.

But I do hear what Hob says before he gets in the car.

"Nobody, my dear," he says. "Nobody at all."

New York City opens up and swallows me whole. The throng of living and dead are even better at masking me than Conroy's shirt, and soon Police Plaza is a memory left far behind. Dorothy's wriggling – must be so annoying being only a head, all those phantom itches – and I want, I need, I must have a drink before I can even think about talking to her. Luckily Manhattan has somewhere in the vicinity of two hundred and fifty million bars – we like a drink around here – and I slip into a place named *Lou's* close to the piers.

It's dark, which suits my mood, and a booth near the back is free. There are too many living people around for the place is up on dead rights, and I'm pretty sure the gorilla at the bar making whiskey sours wouldn't take kindly to a severed head on his bar. I want to talk to Dorothy without drawing any attentio-

"Jonny Faraday. What a pleasant surprise."

Great.

She slides into the booth across from me, swishing against the fake leather. She smells like a side of ham dipped in Chanel no. 5. She's cold, I can feel her from here, so cold she must sleep in a freezer – a dead body can keep cool for as many hours in the day as you keep it just above freezing at night. Helps with the smell. But I can still smell it. Smell her.

"Alison Kastle," I say, dropping Dorothy's bag between my feet. The head squirms but clenching my ankles keeps her trapped.

Dorothy ain't going nowhere.

"With a K," she points out. Again.

"I know."

She gives me that smile, the one where she doesn't show any teeth, that TV smile. You know the one I'm talking about.

She keeps smiling and says, "You still smoking?"

"Gotta die some day."

"Ain't that the truth." She snaps open a cigarette case, draws out a Camel. "Where you been, Jonny? You haven't been returning my phone calls."

She lights the smoke and hands it to me. I say, "I've been busy. Lots to investigate...privately."

"Shame," Kastle purrs. "I thought we had fun that night, you and I. Dead women can go for hours...unlike some living men..."

Great. You fuck a dead woman once and she never lets you live it down.

Dorothy's head is raising a racket – she must be head butting the floor – and from the way Kastle is leaning across the table, she hears it too. "What have you got down there...?"

I slam my ankles together, hoping the move's enough to discourage Dorothy, but all I hit is myself. The head rolls from beneath the table, gets wrapped up in the bag, and comes to rest against Kastle's right shoe. Dorothy looks up at us through a slit in the bag.

Kastle's got class. She takes it as if it's not the first time she's had a dead head at her feet. Who knows, maybe it's not. "You have been busy, Jonny. Who's the head?"

Dorothy gags, her eyes wide. She obviously wants to tell her own story, and since I know it won't freak Kastle out – dead broads know how to keep their cool – but maybe it's time to let the cat out of the bag. Or the head, really.

I pick up the NY bag and take out Dorothy's head.

"About time – fuck! That bag was scratching me up," Dorothy spits. "What are you doing, carrying me around like a piece of meat? Geezus, fuck, man. What were you think-"

I shove Dorothy back inside.

Kastle looks relieved. "Thank God. She always bitch like that?"

"I'm not sure. We haven't been together long."

"You make a cute couple." Kastle's had enough of the foreplay. She moves in for the real action. "She wouldn't, by any chance, belong to the pile of limbs they found under the wheels of the A train?"

The waitress arrives. I order a whiskey, Kastle wants a light beer, and I be nice and get a cherry Coke for Dorothy. With a straw.

"Maybe," I say when the waitress leaves. "What's it to you?"

Kastle sighs. "It's like I always say, Faraday – give and ye shall receive. I want a story and you want....well, I don't think even you know what it is you really want, Jon Faraday. People who aren't afraid of anything think they have nothing to lose. And when you've got nothing to lose, whatever you get is worthless."

"Bit too philosophical, Kastle, for the day I've been having."

The drinks arrive. I knock the whiskey back, liking the way it uncurls warmly in my stomach, and I order another before the waitress leaves. Kastle sips her beer thoughtfully.

"Look," Kastle says, "I know you're onto something, Faraday, and I know it has something to do with the Hampton girl they found in the river. You're working a case, I know it. She's the first dead person this century not to get back up and walk around."

"No shit."

"No, it's not *shit*. This is the biggest story since the Reliving. This is *the* story, Faraday." Kastle sweeps a bang of black hair back from her head. Her hair looks good. Newly Dead hair was the one thing besides fingernails that kept growing. Necros have to dye it, if they want colour. Tends to grey prematurely, necro hair.

"Look, you know as much as I do, Kastle. A girl didn't relive. Big deal. The lifers will love it and the dead rights lot will try to outlaw it without even knowing what it is they're against. Shit like this has been going on in this country since the first flag was flown."

"Not like this," she says. "Haven't you been watching the news?" Kastle stands up, shouts over my shoulder: "Can you turn that up, please?"

The beast cleaning glasses is tamed by the dead beauty and he hits the remote for the TV above the bar. White noise, then:

> ...olice across the boroughs have responded to more than two hundred individual incidents involving lifist crime since the news broke yesterday. This morning, here at the corner of Third Avenue and 47th Street, a Dead Korean hot dog vendor was literally torn to pieces by a mob chanting life supremacist slogans. The man, believed to have relived in his late twenties, is even missing body parts, including his right hand, which has yet to be recovered. Most remarkable of all, however, is that newly dead witnesses report living passersby didn't stop to help the man...And across town at Chelsea Park, a living man and woman have reportedly been attacked by a group of Dead American teenagers. The living man, 42, and woman, 39, sustained injuries to their necks and spines, with neither expected to walk again. Police say the attackers deliberately inflicted injuries that would maim, not kill...

Lifism attacks. I make a mental note to stay away from Chelsea Park.

Kastle, for her part, looks almost pleased. "This city is about to explode, Faraday. Don't you get it? People are losing their minds. It took them two decades to get used to the idea that life goes on when you die, and now the dead don't always come back. That scares a lot of people. All that shit that you sprout, all the shit you say, that everyone else in this fucking city says as well. All that lifist shit is going to burn New York to the ground."

I wish I had more whiskey. "I think you're overreacting," I say.

"Am I?" Kastle asks. "What do you know about Cherry Hampton? Why didn't she relive? Whatever it is, it's not natural. Someone did that to her. If you tell me the truth, I can get put it on the airways and we can stop this before it even begins. Tell me what you know, Jonny. Let me in. Give me the story and you can use me."

"I thought we'd done that dance?"

"Don't be an asshole. The power of the press, Faraday."

I really want to argue with her but the TV catches my eye again. Evelyn Trask, dressed like Jackie O and dabbing at her eyes with a handkerchief. She's surrounded by police officers being walked into a station.

...other news, the wife of prominent Omega America CEO Stephen Trask has been arrested for murder, following the fatal shooting of her husband earlier today. Witnesses report that Evelyn Trask allegedly shot her husband at point blank range at popular Tribeca bistro Vanities earlier today. A spokesperson for Omega said Mr Trask is 'distressed' at the incident and will be cooperating fully with the police. The incident couldn't have come at a worst time for Mr Trask or his company, Omega America, with the shares dropping five points today ahead of what is reportedly a hostile takeover bid by Austere Industries...

Kastle snorts derisively. "Yeah, can you believe it? Face first in the bruschetta, the crazy bitch. I heard a rumor he liked the young ones. Maybe she heard the same thing."

No shit. I start to feel guilty again then I remember I didn't do anything wrong. Sure, providing the evidence that led to a wife killing her husband may not win me a good guy award, but I didn't put the gun in her hand. I didn't pull the trigger. If anything, Trask did it himself. It's not my fault.

Kastle's looks like she's waiting for an answer to a question she doesn't need to ask. It was she who recommended me to Evelyn Trask and she's searching for a story, an angle to attack. I wouldn't give her the satisfaction.

And she can tell this time. Kastle shrugs, stands, slaps a card onto the tabletop. "All right then. Gotta go, Jonny, on a deadline. You call when you've got something for me. We can help each other, Jonny. Remember that."

She walks away, well thought out pumps tacking the floorboards. She doesn't leave any money for the tip or the tab. Oh yeah, I'll call you all right.

I shoot the rest of the whiskey, slide Kastle's beer over. Her pale pink lipstick rims the glass. The beer smells normal when I sniff it, not like formaldehyde or whatever the hell she's using to preserve herself these days. But I still can't drink it. I'm not *that* thirsty.

Chapter 11
Pearls Are a
Nuisance

With Kastle gone I can finally hit the head. Dorothy's settled so I take her out of the bag.

"I'm sick of being in there," she says. Who'd have thought a decapitated head could look so haughty?

"Fine," I say, "but you have to keep it down. *Lou's* is one of the more respectable bars I frequent and I'd hate to have my VIP membership revoked."

She does me the honor of laughing, though not much. I put the straw in her Coke, maneuvering it so she can drink. Most of the soda ends up leaking on the table through the stitches Conroy made in Dorothy's neck. But drinking seems to relax her. Makes her feel more human.

I decide to start slowly. "I know you know more than you're letting on."

Dorothy looks confused. "What?"

"Let me rephrase – when I showed you the picture of Cherry, you said you didn't know her. But you do, don't you?"

She doesn't answer and it takes me a moment to realise she's trying to nod.

"Yes or no will do, Dorothy."

"Yeah." She looks stricken. "I didn't tell you earlier because I thought I'd get into trouble...from Cyrus."

93

"Tell me about her."

"Cherry? We met at the Skeleton, few weeks back,
shared a shift when it got busy, before...um, Cyrus hired
her. Said he met her at the park. She knew all of Cyrus'
other girls too, the one who came into the bar."

"Cyrus ran girls?"

Dorothy goes quiet. I don't know if it's the fact
she's just a head or not, but I feel more than my usual lack
of sympathy. "I didn't mean you, Dorothy."

She gives me a grateful grin. "Yeah. Cyrus was a
pimp. He...he did try to get me into tricks, said I could
make more money if I did. And I thought about it. I was
going to school, tuition costs, you know. But I couldn't
look at myself if I did. Not Cherry, though.
Cherry...there was something wrong with her. I'd see her
sometimes, working the other side of the bar – she didn't
mix drinks, even though he said she worked there. She'd
be talking up the tricks from her favourite spot, the corner
booth beneath the moose head. Cyrus liked her, I think.
At least he treated her a bit better than he did the other
girls."

"How so?"

"I don't know. Just seemed like he wanted to keep
her...*clean*. He wouldn't sell her to just anyone. Like this
one time, this guy came in, big mean looking black guy,
looking for a blonde girl. Cherry was the only one Cyrus
had working that night and he still wouldn't let the black
guy have her. Said he was saving her. I think Cherry
liked that. Being saved."

Dorothy slurps her Coke. Some more of the liquid
seeps out through her stitches, like she's shedding black,
bubbly blood. "You know she was rich, right? Cherry, she
told me her dad had so much money he could swim in it,
like that duck in that comic book. Scrooge McDuck!
Yeah, she said he was so rich... I don't know what she was
doing in the Skeleton, what she was doing with Cyrus. If

you were that rich, why would you stay there? I wouldn't, that's for sure."

It's depressing when a severed head gets morose, so I try to change the subject. "She lived at the bar?"

"Yeah. Upstairs in Cyrus' apartment. That was weird, though. Cyrus always had a thing for dead girls more than living ones. Everyone in the bar was real surprised when he let her stay at his place."

Cyrus liked them dead, huh? Maybe he had plans for Cherry beyond her salvation. I ask Dorothy, "Was there ever anyone interested in Cherry? Besides the usual Johns at the bar?"

Dorothy looks as thoughtful as a decapitated head can look. "I don't remem...hang on. There was this one guy. Came around once, talked to Cyrus. I noticed him because he dressed different to all the other guys Cyrus used to talk to. A really nice suit, like you see in the windows of Armani or something. I'm guessing this guy had money.

"This day he came around, Cherry looks all scared all of a sudden, and she and Cyrus hustled him outside. I...well, I wasn't eavesdropping or nothing, but when I took out the trash, the three of them were in the alley and the guy in the suit was talking real loud and Cyrus was between him and Cherry. The suit kept trying to grab Cherry's arm, like he wanted her to come with him, but she kept pulling away. Cherry was angry, too, more angry than the guy. She looked tired, like what she was saying she'd said a million times. I didn't stay outside long and when Cherry and Cyrus came in, the guy in the suit wasn't with them."

"Who's the guy?"

"Never seen him before, don't know."

"When was this?"

"Probably, oh, a week ago. That was the last time I saw Cherry, too. She came back into the bar and sat at her booth. She looked all scared, crying and shaking. She was reading something and she scrunched it up when I came and asked her if she wanted a drink. She...she told me I'd been good to her, that she always thought of me as a friend. It was weird, you know?

"My...mom...died of stomach cancer and she knew....she knew she didn't have long to go. What Cherry said...she sounded like my mom did. Like she knew something was coming...something bad.

"Cherry went up to the apartment with Cyrus just before my shift finished. By the time I was done, they hadn't come down, and I never saw Cherry again until you turned up with that photo of her."

Answers start to form. Cyrus finds blonde runaway Cherry, wants to keep her for himself. Young, impressionable, bitter rich bitch meets Greenwich wannabe gangster. The gangster finds his stake is sweeter, which attracts a higher class bee. Did he sell her to the highest bidder? The guy with the money clothes? Did he get too rough? Did he kill her? And if he did, why didn't she relive? What's the unknown substance he pumped into her? The answers are just giving me more questions, which are giving me a headache.

I ask Dorothy if she's finished her cherry Coke, then where I can drop her.

She goes all doe-eyed. Not easy when your eyes are dead white. "Can't I stay with you?"

"It would never work between us," I say. "I'm a leg man."

"What, so that's it? I'm a severed head. You can't just leave me at a bus stop."

She seems pretty okay for someone who just died but this is her way of dealing. Soon enough she'll be interviewed by a homicide detective for a few hours while a horny CSI guy dusts her for prints. Then she'll have the hassle of sorting her limbs from Charlie's before she has to drag all the pieces down to City Hall to verify that she's Newly Dead so her bank accounts won't be frozen. She's lost her job for sure now, since she'll have to tell the cops about Cyrus and his business will be seized, so the best she'll be able to do is flip burgers at McDonald's. Yep. There was plenty of time left for Dorothy to mourn.

She's mourning now, as much as Newly Dead can. I touch her cheek in my own stunted attempt at consoling her. It's not like I can hug her. I'd be covered with Coke.

Dorothy's blubbering, hitching. She doesn't know she can't really cry. "Y-you think...you think what...what killed Cherry...you think that could happen to me?"

Her eyes tell me she wishes it would. Every so often I want to give hope to other people. It's a fleeting feeling and I tend to run with it. "Definitely. Sure."

She gives me a cracked smile. Everyone seems to think death – final, irrevocable death – is somehow more agreeable than being Newly Dead. We all see how the dead live, how the living treat them. We all know we're going to be dead someday, but we still look down on anyone without a pulse. And then, when we do die, when *we* relive, we see the world through dead eyes and we just want to die all over again. So pointless. No wonder Dorothy wants out.

I offer to drive Dorothy to the nearest precinct but she spies Kastle's business card floating in a puddle of undigested cherry Coke. "Nah. Just call that reporter for me, willya? Tell her I have a story she might be interested in." She's bouncing back – no mean feat for a head.

I put the call to Kastle. Get voicemail. I tell her I'm giving her head – what do I get in return? And I tell her she better hurry before someone mistakes Dorothy for a necro love toy and takes her home.

Chapter 12
Pickup on Noon
Street

Greenwich Village is a walk from here but I can't seem to remember where I parked my car. Maybe I do have concussion...

So I take another cab. Or at least I try to and fail, due to the traffic damming up on Broadway. Walking's the only option.

There's a street market near the Downtown Hospital and I really want a different shirt than the Hawaiian from Conroy. The little stall's selling cheap sunglasses and weird masks – heaps of masks, stacked in a loose pile up against the chain link fence of a carpark – and the vendor is trying to flog a sleeping mat to a pair of Dead Swedes, backpackers by the look of them. The dead pair, a Hans and a Heidi for sure, are shaking the vendor off, Heidi smiling as she backs away. She doesn't see the living man she's about to walk into.

Heidi and the living man bounce off each other. "Watch out, zombie bitch," the living man says, clutching his briefcase to his chest as if Dead Swedish backpackers were known for rolling stockbrokers.

"What did you say?" Hans is angry.

The living guy eyes Hans' burly arms, tries to walk away. "You heard me, necro."

Next thing I know the living man's on his ass, the dead backpacker standing over him while his girlfriend tries to hold him back. Normally that would be it – who would be fool enough to stand up to a dead man the size of Hans? – but something's different today.

The necro kid outside the McDonalds, the dead hot dog vendor with the missing hand, the news report of the couple with broken necks in the park. Maybe Kastle was right. Maybe it was all coming to a head.

"You can't talk to me like that, you, you FUCKING corpse!" the living man squeals. Middle age spread quivers as he struggles to stand.

"What's going on here?" A beat cop steps in, brandishing his authority like a swinging dick, the armpits of his uniform stained yellow by sweat. The aura of power is as strong as the hot dog relish on his breath. "You making trouble?" he puts to the necro tourist.

"That THING assaulted me," the business man snaps. "I will be pressing CHARGES, officer." He's one of those guys who have the annoying habit of saying certain words louder than others.

The Dead Swede's a blunt trauma victim by the look, the back of his skull's been caved in and put back together. He swells his dead, yet formidable chest and says, "I did not hit first."

The cop's coming towards the Dead Swede, hand resting on the grip of his gun, handcuffs in the other. "I don't care who started it, you're coming with me."

"Why him, huh?" ask a Dead Asian American woman standing nearby. "I saw. He do nothing. Other, live man, he start fight."

"Quiet, ma'am," the beat cop says. His voice is still crisp, still certain - but it has an edge now, that cops put on when a member of the public questions them. I've done the same thing, many times. Most of the time it works. But it's not working today.

"You no tell me quiet, you no tell me," the Dead woman harangues. She's pointing a finger at the officer, as if she's jabbing him with a needle. "I have rights, I have rights, I talk, you listen."

The business man joins in: "Shut up, neccer."

There's a collective gasp from the crowd. I curse the luck that I keep having, to find myself in the middle of this.

The cop is caught. I know he's heard nothing but *dead rights this, dead rights that* from his commander, the PR suits from the NYPD, even the commissioner. He knows that if he ends up with lifism charges laid against him, that's the sort of thing that can follow you into your afterlife. Permanent records are a lot more permanent these days.

But the cop looks like he's taken more than his share. "Look, lady, back off. You!" He swings the handcuffs at the Dead Swede. "I don't care what she says, you're coming with me. Hands behind your back."

The crowd mutters. It's seething, the mistrust and disgust and misplaced thoughts roiling. There's enough Newly Dead in the mob to make me wish I was one of them. If this powder keg erupts, the living won't get off so easy this time.

The cop steps to the Swede. "Hands behind your back!" His finger's itching to pull his gun but at least he's level headed enough to realise it wouldn't do any good. He's still hoping his voice will be enough.

The Swede has years of being treated like a piece of dead meat etched into his face clearer than his stitches. Heidi looks like she would cry if she could.

"Put your fucking hands behind your back, neccer!" And there's the match.

The Dead Asian American woman cries: "You lifist, you lifist pig, lifist pig!"

"I told YOU to shut up, dead bitch," the business

man says.

"You shut up, you fucking lifist!" someone says.

"Fucking dead, think they own the world!" someone else says.

"What do you know, hey? You don't know what it's like."

"Bullshit. All I hear is how tough the dead have it. Well, wake up call – living ain't that easy, either."

"Yeah."

"Lifist pig!"

"You can't talk to ME like that!"

"Fucking necros!"

"Hey, you'll be one soon enough."

"You threatening me?"

"You heard me, motherfucker."

The crowd's a mob, splitting down the centre between the living and the dead. The cop's smart enough to realise he can't control this. He's talking rapid-fire into his radio when a 7-Eleven Big Gulp, half full of what looks like Mountain Dew, flies by his head. "Hey! Who threw that?"

"Fucking dead should all be burnt up. Ain't right, it ain't right..."

"Kill 'em all!"

"Kick 'em out of our country!"

"America mine too!"

"How many times do I have to TELL you to shut up, NECCER BITCH?"

Screaming like a banshee, the Dead Asian American woman launches herself at the business man. She hits him and he sprawls in a heap of dead limbs, and although she's stick-thin, he can't fight her off as she pummels his face.

The cop grabs her around the middle – "Off of him, neccer, off!" – and he almost succeeds before Heidi the Dead Swede hits him in the back of the head with her bag.

A living man, bulbous fat, steps up and kicks Heidi in the gut, sending her flailing, but Hans the Dead Swede saw the hit and he slams into the fat man.

You can tell where this is going.

The crowd erupts, dead versus living, and lucky Jon Faraday's right in the middle. A Newly Dead man in a Knicks hat tries to wrestle me but a living woman who looks like Oprah Winfrey gets in the way and he falls on her like a rat sniffing sugar. The business man, the lifist jerk who started this whole thing, has his arm pinned behind his back by the dead woman, and she's screaming, spitting, biting at his face.

Something or someone hits me in the back, sending searing pain through my tender shoulder, and I'm spun around. A dead teenager slaps me across the face with one of the weird masks from the street stall and I fall. African death gods dance like little pygmies before my eyes. For a moment I lose it.

All sound leaks away and there's only the ringing in my ears. I'm on the ground, looking up. Dead and living fight above me, around me, on top of me. All around me there's someone beating a dead person, a necro punching a living person; but for now I can see blue sky and white clouds through the gap my fall has made.

There's a noise through the muted air. A little Newly Dead girl, grey pigtails, face ashen and stripped with burn marks as if she died in some raging inferno. She's not crying – the dead don't have tears – but she remembers how, and the look of anguish on her little, dead face brings the world crashing back.

I can't stand, I'd be too much of a target, so I crawl, push, pull my way through the forest of living and dead legs. The heel of an Italian leather pump grazes my cheek, a detached hand makes a grab for my leg. The Dead Asian American woman hollers: "Me live here! Me live here!" and I really, really hope the meaty thumps I'm hearing are the living business man's head connecting with the pavement. Repeatedly.

Freedom's in sight, a clearing in the leg forest, but I can't reach it because someone's picking me up by the scruff of my shirt.

I'm face to face with the Dead Swede, the fury in his dull eyes a storm waiting to strike, when a shrill whistle cuts the air. The beat cop's call for backup. He must have gotten through.

Something metal and round tumbles into the crowd and explodes with light and gas, scattering the rioters and felling more than a couple. I'm blinded and the air is rife with something acidic. I've smelt this before. CS gas. A fucking tear gas grenade.

But this one's different to the standard crowd pleaser because it's also half a flash bang grenade. NYPD call them everymans, because the gas fucks up the living as much as the light fucks up the dead.

The Dead Swede's preoccupied with the fact his brain's temporarily shut down and I can't see properly. I stumble, I trip, I need to get away. There are vague shapes in the gas clouds, shapes that might be people, but they could just be the spots dancing before my eyes.

Nope. Must be people. Spots usually don't swing night sticks.

Chapter 13
The Jury

I wake up in Downtown Hospital. I know this because Brenda Barrett tells me. It's the first thing she says. Not *hello* or *how are you feeling?* She must be pissed.

I can see why. The emergency room looks like the Day of the Dead. Bruised and battered New Yorkers, blood splattered bandages, cuts and scrapes. A Dead American fingers his tie, his throat a deep blue as if he died choking on a cocktail onion. A living tennis player gazes apologetically at his girlfriend as she dabs his grazed elbows and knees with a cloth. A fat woman sneezes and glances around, eyes rheumy. A dead teenage girl glares sourly as she sits beside her mother; I can see the rope burn on her neck and her mother won't meet her eyes.

Funny, most of the people are Newly Dead. I don't know what they're doing here. Hospitals are for the living. There's nothing here that can help them now.

A few of the dead are recognizable from the crowd near the street market on Broadway. Some have actually lost limbs and cradle their busted arms and legs in their laps. They look as if they're wondering if their insurance policy covers reattaching body parts. I know HMO doesn't.

Can't see the little necro girl with grey pigtails. I hope she's okay.

My chin is warm with blood and I've got a broken nose. Brenda Barrett shoves an ice pack at me and crosses her arms. I try not to voice the irony of my ex-wife giving me cold water *and* the cold shoulder at the same time, and ask her why she's here.

"You haven't changed your medical records, *Jon*." I don't like the way she accentuates my name. Like a curse. "I'm still your next of kin."

"It's on my to-do list," I say.

My nose makes it hard to breathe, so I grasp it and tug, cracking the bone back into place. Hurts like hell but at least it stops the bleeding. Brenda's looking at me as if I just farted in church. The ice pack is as comforting as my ex-wife.

A TV set in the corner shows a Dead Rights march somewhere in Harlem by the looks. The necro protestors walk silently, holding candles and banners that say AFTERLIFE IS STILL LIFE and GOD MADE ME TO GO AND GO AND GO. They could be protesting anything but it's probably got more to do with Cherry Hampton not reliving than the new legislation against dead marriages.

"How's Ray?" I don't really care but I like the guilt. When your wife leaves you for your partner – and both become your exes – you can afford to be a selfish asshole. I say.

"Fine," and the way she says it tells me so much. We were married, and I know what Brenda Barrett means when she says *fine*. She used to say that about us.

"Must be hard for *Detective* Gannon," I say, "sleeping with a woman who defends the biggest zombie mobster in New York."

Brenda tightens her lips at the mention of Ole Hob. "My client is not-"

"Save it for the sound bites, I've had too bad a day for bullshit."

"That was always your problem, Jon." Here we go. "You think you should be spared because you've had *a bad day*. Open your eyes. You're not the only one in New York having a bad day."

Leave it to an ex-wife to point out your shortcomings, even when you're in an emergency room.

Brenda's staring at me, I can see her from the corner of my eye. She asks: "You're still thinking about that girl, aren't you?"

At first I think she's talking about Cherry. But she's not. She means that damn bar in Tribeca five years ago. She means the girl I found with Gray Gary J.

"No."

"Now who's lying?"

I remember why we didn't work. She always knew me a little too well.

"Okay," I concede, "maybe I am. But what's it to you? You didn't want to know then and you don't want to know now."

Something seems to let go inside her and she slumps a little. No mean feat in the suit she's wearing. "I did want to know," she sighs. "It was you who didn't want to talk."

"Horseshit."

She flares up, just like old times. "God, I knew this would happen. The whole way down here I thought – I hoped! – we could talk. But you're still a child. You still think you're the only one who got hurt and that *I* did the hurting. Do you remember that night, after it all went down? You remember what happened when you came home? I do. You wouldn't look at me, wouldn't come near me. Wouldn't touch me. You were a ghost."

"It's a dead world, Brenda. Ghosts, zombies. What do you expect?"

"I expect my husband to talk to me when he has a problem, not shut me out. It's no wonder I..."

"What? Fucked my partner?"

That instant of softness is gone when I say the words. A small part of me is pleased. Another part is calling me an asshole.

"I came down here because the hospital said you were hurt. How stupid of me. As if anything could hurt the great Jon Faraday."

Brenda stands stiffly. She doesn't look at me. "Change your next of kin, Jon. I don't want them calling me when you die."

She goes to walk away, stylish pumps tacking the age-worn linoleum. But she can't leave yet; I have to know what she was doing in the morgue earlier today.

"What's your interest in Cyrus Beaumont?"

The question stops her mid-stride. "How...what do you mean?"

"A little birdie told me you've been checking into his lack of afterlife," I say. "I'm guessing you did so at the request of a client. And I can also guess which one."

"What are you getting at?"

I struggle out of the chair. "C'mon, Brenda. Don't dance around me, I'm not in a court room. Why don't you just assume I know you're checking it out and cut the bullshit?"

She finally faces me. All-business Brenda is back. "I was merely making discrete inquiries. Discrete. Not a word your crime lab buddy knows a lot about, hmm?"

I shrug. "Maybe not, but I've got a reputation for it, apparently. What does Ole Hob have to do with Cyrus?"

"My client has been implicated – falsely, I might add – in the murder of Cyrus Beaumont. As his lawyer, I was looking into the case on his behalf and attempting to stop the rumor mill before it started turning."

"How was Hob implicated?"

She's trying to decide how much to tell me. "Falsely," she says, as if that's enough. I hate lawyers.

They lie better than criminals.

"They knew each other?"

Brenda purses her lips. "As far as I'm aware...no."

She watches her words. If I was Grandpa Hob's lawyer, there'd be certain things I wouldn't want to know either. Selective reality, Brenda used to call it. You only want to know as much as you need to get your client off whatever charge is being leveled at that time. Anything else and you might find your attorney-client privilege wavering along with your resolve.

"Okay. Are you aware, then, that Cyrus ran the girl who washed up dead at Carl Schulz Park? The one who didn't relive?"

A raised eyebrow. She's genuinely surprised. "No."

I'm starting to wonder if she's dodging the questions because she doesn't know, or whether she just doesn't want *me* to know. "Didn't Ray mention her? Or Hob?"

She goes colder, if that's possible. "No."

"You don't really know much, do you?"

"You're the one with the questions, Jon."

"All I know is the girl, Cherry, worked for Cyrus Beaumont and both of them turned up dead. One from an overdose of something strong enough that she didn't come back, the other because he knew something about her and someone didn't want him to talk, so they burnt his face off with acid. Who does that sound like if not Grandpa Hob, the neccer kingpin of Harlem?"

Brenda shakes her head. "Still trying to save dead girls, Jon. You haven't changed at all."

I slump back in the chair. She's not going to tell me. It's like we're married all over again.

But at least there's a modicum of affection when she asks, "What do you care? Really, Jon – what do you care?"

I can't answer.

"See?" she says as she walks away. "That's why I left you. You never could talk to me."

I don't watch her leave but even over the noise of the emergency room I can hear her heels tapping towards the door. Who would have thought shoes could be so recriminating?

Brenda. You're so right. What do I care?

I don't bother trying to see a doctor – he can't cure what I've got anyway – so I leave.

Night's falling. Even if I couldn't see it, I could smell it, as if the wind changes when the sun's done and the breeze off the Hudson brings a city of steam and sweat to my nose. Or maybe I'm just imagining that I can smell New York more at night, that her stench only truly blossoms in the shadows.

Wow. I think that tear gas really fucked me up.

I've had enough of today so I head for home. But a pack of z-boys in the back of a *New York Times* truck have other ideas.

The gangbangers are tearing up the street in the stolen van, throwing newspapers and abuse at any living they see, most of who shrink back and hurry away. I've never been any good at shrinking or running and I'm only vaguely aware that I should get off the street. Usually these Newly Dead keep to Morningside, robbing 7-11s and shooting each other over turf. Obviously the shit going down in the Big Apple has stirred them up.

One of the young neccers, his head a mess of spiky grey hair and metal sutures, spots me. "Catch!" he hollers as he hurls a stack of newspapers at my head.

It hits like a brick.

Chapter 14
Bay City Blues

I swim in darkness until consciousness seeps back in.
Groan. Open my eyes. They're gummy but serviceable.
I'm getting sick of being knocked out.

I'm propped up against the sign for the Canal Street
Station, sitting on the pigeon shit splattered trim of the
station sign. If I strain I can just see a Grolsch ad above
me mocking about the good life. And I can also see Alison
Kastle.

She's standing over me, a corpse in a
Bloomingdale's suit. She combs the hair back from my
forehead with a dead, hot pink fingernail. "How are you
feeling, Jonny?"

Her sympathy irks me. "Wh...wh...what...?"
Obviously the *New York Times* have done me more harm
then good. I can't seem to talk. Maybe Kastle's right.
Maybe I do need to watch the news more. Or at least get
out of its way.

"What's a nice girl like me doing with a guy like
you?" Kastle prompts.

A fire truck blares by, a streak of sound and light.
Where's he going in such a hurry?

I shake my head, flicking away her hand. I'm in no
mood for anyone's humor but my own. "N-no. What-
what are you doing here?"

Kastle frosts up. "There's stuff going down

everywhere in the city tonight, Jonny. I heard another riot had broken out, Broadway and Walker, so I came running. By the time we got through the traffic it was all over. NYPD blue were arresting everyone walking, living or dead. Heard they're just taking them in and then letting them go. No arrest, nothing. No room at the inn, am I right? Anyway, we're coming back and who should I see lying in a pool of his own blood?"

"Your father?" Her DNBC News van is parked at the curb. Terry, Kastle's cameraman, waves to me from the cab. He looks bored.

She snorts. "Funny." She sniffs. "Makes me wonder why I bothered to ask Terry to drag your ass off the street."

I do a stock take, find some nice new bruises to go with the old ones from the last few days. But I can still stand, I'm getting better at talking, and those questions are still nibbling away at me. I guess I'll be fine.

"How'd you like the head? Good for you?" I ask. Yep. The wit's working fine, too.

"I've had worse," Kastle deadpans. Easier to pull off when you are dead. "Dorothy told me you were looking into Cherry Hampton's suicide."

"Suicide? What are you talking about?"

She steps to the news van. "Jonny – you really need to watch the news more." Kastle slides the door open with a practiced motion. Inside the truck there's a bank of black Sony monitors, sound equipment and lots and lots of dials. She explained to me once what all this stuff did. I wasn't really listening. Thankfully there's no pop quiz today.

"Where's Dorothy? I thought she'd be with you."

"Dropped her at the ninth precinct. She was pretty shook up by the time I'd finished with her."

"Shook up? Must have been tough for a head. Still, nothing like opening wounds for a good story, huh?"

Kastle shrugs unapologetically. "It's what I do."

She sits in the console chair, flicks a switch, and four of the small televisions set in the wall wink to life. Images fill the screens, streaming from DNBC, Bloomsbury, some yokel affiliate channel from Kansas, and even the BBC. They all look the same. People, alive and dead, and they're doing either one of three things: Fighting. Running. Or praying.

"That fire I told you about? Looks like it's spreading." Kastle points to one of the screens, toggles a switch with her other hand. "But you don't care about that, do you? Here, then. Here's the latest on Cheryl Hampton."

Images of a gang of young dead throwing bricks and stones at a church in Morningside are replaced with a shot of Kastle herself standing in front of Police Plaza. Cut to my bestest buddy Detective Ray Gannon doing a press conference, his tie so tight he looks constipated. Kastle reaches to turn the volume dial but I stop her. I don't really want to hear his voice.

"The cops said she killed herself?" I ask.

"Yep," Kastle says. "Self-inflicted relive. 'Course, she didn't technically relive, so I guess it's a moot point. What do you think?"

My face must be mirroring my thoughts. Kastle notes my skepticism. I am laying it on pretty thick.

"Yeah. I don't buy it either," she says. "Dorothy said Cherry wouldn't have killed herself and I believe her. Cops said the autopsy showed an armful of heroin and half the river floating in her gut. Funny...but since the cops put this out, do you know how many dead people there are swimming in the East River? Some have got it into their heads that the river's sacred. You should see the water off Randall-Ward Island – like the Ganges, the amount of newly dead swimming out there. Crazy what people believe in. Speaking of which, I spoke to your friend

Francis – he's a strange one, isn't he? Told me the autopsy report was bogus and he never signed off on the heroin. Off the record, of course."

"He told me *substance unknown*," I say. Francis. Conroy must use his first name with the ladies.

Kastle nods. "I got the impression he didn't know. And that he's a necrophiliac." No wonder he's a friend of yours."

Cute. I change the subject: "Got a phone?"

She reaches into her handbag and tosses me a cell phone, saying: "Who you calling?"

"The zombie-loving CSI."

"Good luck. Police are so stretched across the city I heard they're even pulling in the coastguard and putting them on the streets. It's only a matter of time before martial law's declared. You're not going to get through to the Plaza."

She's right. The phone's a dead tone. As an experiment, I dial 911. No answer either, just a recorded message telling me all operators are busy. Shit. The world is burning.

I hand the cell phone back to Kastle but she waves me off. "Keep it. At least it might mean you'll call me sometime."

I slide the cell into my pocket and wish I still had my gun. No point asking Kastle for one – but she can give me a ride.

A minute later we're heading up Broadway, Terry gunning the newsvan through holes in the traffic. I'm in the back, clinging to the console chair and trying to sort the wheat from the chaff. Mentally, of course. Hard work, considering what I have to go on, with all the questions and not a hell of a lot of answers.

I still think Cyrus' place is as good a shot as any. Cherry Hampton was missing for at least a week before she turned up in the river. Dorothy said Cherry had been staying in Cyrus' apartment. There might be something there to go on.

We're speeding through Soho when Terry slams on the brakes. "Hold on!" he says tightly, but of course I've let go of the chair at this moment. He spins the wheel and I'm thrown into the Sony equipment. It hurts.

"What the fuck?" Terry's as eloquent as ever.

"Look at that, Terry! Shoot it, shoot it!" Kastle is chanting.

I drag myself to the front of the van. Kastle's so excited I think her head's going to fall off, while Terry has a handheld camera and he's filming right up against the windscreen. Through the glass is Vesuvio's Bakery. Usually the front window is filled with French loaves, lined up like severed fingers stacked by a serial killer. But tonight the little green bakery looks like something out of Fight Club.

People whale on each other with pipes, baseball bats, whatever they can find. Dead, living, looters or rioters, the mob is a mix that blurs before my eyes. I can't tell the difference between them. I can't tell who's right and who's wrong and I can't decide who I want to win.

Terry is almost salivating as his camera soaks up the violence, and Kastle is clenching Terry's shoulder so hard she's drawing blood. Maybe, in something like this, Kastle is the only one who really wins.

The dead, detached arm of one of the fighters lands on the hood of the van with a solid thump. The arm scrabbles at the wipers, clawing the windscreen.

"Jesus," Kastle says, sounding awed. "Tell me you got that, Terry."

"Oh yeah."

The van rocks on its shocks and the driver's side window shatters in a spray of glass. A dead man, I can't tell what type, he could be Dead Armenian or a Dead Italian, they all look the same now, a dead man is shoving another man's head through the van's window. He's hollering while he does it, but not words, no, there's no sense to what he's saying.

"SHIT!" Terry reels back, his face stained with blood from the man's slit throat.

"Go, go, GO!" I scream.

Terry, resolve broken, pops the clutch and guns away from the curb. The cameraman's face is covered with blood and he claws at his eyes, the steering wheel running loose without his control.

The dead man is still holding the man he just killed and for a second his dull eyes bring him back to reality. Just in time for the van to hit the gutter and pop him and his victim free. They scrape down the side of the van and then there's a thud when they go under the back wheel.

We're about to hit a new age bookstore – for an instant I contemplate just letting it happen – then Kastle screams, "BRAKE! BRAKE!" and I reach over Terry, grab the wheel and pull. The cameraman hits the pedal and we screech to a stop within inches of breaking the front window. The bookstore is saved. Pity.

Terry is freaked out, rubbing at the blood on his face with a weird, twitchy motion, and even Kastle looks pale.

There's a tapping on the windscreen and as one we all look up to see the dead arm still holding grimly to one of the wipers. I lean over and flick the switch. The wiper swipes the arm from the windscreen and the dead appendage flops to the pavement. Without a word, we drive off.

We reach Greenwich Village and I hop out and finally remember where my car is. Right here. I slide the van door closed and Kastle leans out the driver's side window. "You're welcome," she says.

"Yeah, yeah, thanks for the ride." She stares. I know what's going through her dead brain. "And yeah, I'll call you when I have something."

Her smile would chill an Eskimo. "Good boy. Take care of yourself, Jonny. You'll be dead soon enough and the afterlife's better if you look after yourself while you're alive."

The newsvan rolls away and I curse that I didn't have the last word. Next time, Kastle. Next time.

Chapter 15 smart
Aleck Kill

Greenwich is quieter than I thought it would be, but the area has gone more cosmopolitan lately, rich young couples and all that. What was happening in Soho must be keeping a lot of people off the streets in Greenwich, safe behind their expensive locks. I wonder how long they'll last. The locks and the rich young couples.

The cell phone in my pocket rings and it takes me a while to realise it's mine. The ringtone is *Holiday in Cambodia* by the Dead Kennedys. Ha ha, Kastle. I flick open the phone and say hello.

"Mr Faraday? Evelyn Trask."

Weird. I thought she was in jail. "Mrs Trask. How...are you?"

"You mean except for the fact that I'm in jail...fine. I just got your number off Alison Kastle. They're letting me use the phone to call my lawyer but I wanted to call you first and let you know about the pictures I saw on your camera. Not the ones of Stephen, but the other photographs you took. Of the girl."

She means the shots of Cherry Hampton down by the river. What does she know?

"I had your camera on me when I was arrested, and the detectives asked me about the pictures of the blonde girl during the first interview. I said it was a friend's

117

camera - I left your name out, I hope that's okay - and I told them I'd never seen her before in my life." She pauses for dramatic effect. "I lied, Mr Faraday. I have seen her before. Or at least, I'd seen a picture of her.

"I was in Stephen's office, oh, a week ago I guess, when I accidentally knocked over a pile of folders. All sorts of paper came out - reports, forms, I couldn't make any sense of it - but what I did see were photographs, like mug shots. Of the blonde girl on your camera, and other children.

"Mr Faraday - in the photographs...the children were Newly Dead."

What the? I stop walking, cradle the phone tightly against my cheek. What was a file on Cherry Hampton doing in Stephen Trask's home office? Who are the other children and why are they dead? Hang on - did she say *all* of the children?

"Was...was the blonde girl dead in the photo?" I ask.

Evelyn sniffs. "Not as far as I could tell but the others definitely were. Who was she, Mr Faraday?"

I don't want to go into the whole story, so I say: "Someone a lot like you, Evelyn. A woman fucked over by powerful men."

We hang up after I tell her to hold in there – she laughed at that, a sound like fingernails scraping a tombstone – and I'm starting to see connections I haven't seen before. Stephen Trask and Cherry, Stephen Trask and Cherry. Trask is the head honcho of a pharmaceutical giant that the news said was slowly going down the toilet. Cherry is a runaway killed by a drug the FDA has no knowledge of.

Answers to those questions are coming, I can feel them. I'm hoping Cyrus Beaumont's apartment can give me more to go on.

The Closet Skeleton is dark against the lights of

Greenwich. Nobody home. The police tape's still there, a band of yellow wrapping the front door. I remember the alley the Arnie twins took me into – when was that, only this morning? Feels like weeks and weeks of pain ago – and I remember the fire escape that had been just out of reach while fists the size of planets robbed me of consciousness. Maybe the fire escape would help me this time.

The alley's deserted. I stand on the edge of a Dumpster and I can reach the ladder. In no time I'm scaling the side of the building to the apartment.

No light through the window, nobody around. I jimmy the lock. No use. So I use a potted plant that looked like it died around the start of the century, and break the window. A dog barks somewhere but that's it. No lights, no one calls out, no one comes running. Sometimes I really love living in New York. For a city that never sleeps it's amazing what you can get away with at night.

Cyrus Beaumont's apartment is stylish, tasteful and cleaner then mine. Maybe I should have been a pimp instead of a PI. Obviously pays better and I'm sure the perks more than make up for.

I search the place. Bed, ruffled black silk sheets, oversize picture of a naked woman on the wall. Classy. Wardrobe, big. Suits, good brands. Where was Cyrus getting all his cash? The bar couldn't bring in that much. Who was paying him and what was he doing to earn it? I run my hand along the clothes. Nothing for a woman. Where were Cherry's things? The lounge is one of those coldly modern affairs, sleek lines and strange shaped cushions. Kitchen, bathroom – nothing weird there. Magazines, unopened bills in Cyrus' name on the hall stand. Nothing. Not a sign of Cherry Hampton.

I slump on the couch. Was Dorothy wrong? Except for the ruffled sheets, you'd swear only Cyrus lived here. The wardrobe's only got his clothes. There is no place in this apartment for Cherry.

Shit.

Look, it's not as if I'm just expecting a clue to jump out and go: "Hey, check me out! I'm a clue!" Not really. It's just that it would make my life a hell of a lot easier. But life wasn't meant to be easy, isn't that what they always say? Life or death.

The events of the day have taken their toll. I could probably curl up on Cyrus' couch right now and sleep for twenty hours. But even with everything's that happened to me - or maybe because of it - I'm filled with nervous energy and I have to use it while it's inside me.

I go out the way I came in and I'm a bit preoccupied on the way down the fire ladder. So much so that my grip goes on the third rung from the bottom and I end up falling into the Dumpster. Great. Trash cushions my drop and provides an all too real metaphor for my day.

But as I pick banana peel out of my hair, I see it. That clue I was telling you about.

There's a window of The Closet Skeleton at eye level with the Dumpster, and through the soot stained glass I can just make out a stuffed moosehead tacked to the wall of the bar. Moosehead. What was it Dorothy said?

Cherry would talk up the tricks from her favourite spot, the head had said. *The corner booth beneath the moosehead.*

A minute later I'm back in to the apartment. There's a door I didn't go through before and a set of stairs leading down, the key to the door at the bottom conveniently hanging from a nail. The Skeleton smells like wet smoke, and the white police tap outlining the spot where Cyrus bought the farm seems to glow from the light coming from the street. Thankfully the corner booth was too far from the fire to catch alight, and I take a seat.

There's nothing under the table when I run my hand beneath it, around it, over it. The booth's plush but faded, the outer layer tight against the cushion. The moosehead looks as old as Grandpa Hob. I frisk it, nothing. I even check inside the mouth. My hand goes in up to the wrist. Nada. The moose's dead eyes glare at me.

I slump. Some clue, Faraday. A wild moose chase more like it.

I stand up and there's a sound at my feet. Like crumpled paper. The heel of my left boot's caught something stuck under the bottom of the booth, the corner of a piece of paper just poking out. I pull it free gently and catch sight of a letterhead. Glaring at me is this:

$$\Omega$$

For an instant I'm back beside the river last night, looking at a pale, dead, unmoving ankle and a newly scarred tattoo. I thought it was a number two when I saw it, but it was only half-finished. A half-finished, homemade tattoo, something you'd do with a pin and pen ink, something done in desperation in a dark, dark place.

Below the symbol are the words:

OMEGA INSTITUTE

It's everywhere I go. Omega.

The paper looks like an admittance report for a hospital. A whole lot of jargon that means nothing, statistics and read outs from tests. And then it jumps out – an even better clue.

Patient: Cheryl Maree Hampton

Cherry.

But the kicker is what's at the bottom. On the left is the name of the admitting doctor – a Dr Xin Chan – and on the right is a signature I've seen once before. It's the signature of the man who wrote me a retainer check a week ago.

Douglas Hampton III.

I'm on the cell phone as soon as I clear the alley. If Hampton signed this report, that means he had his daughter admitted. I can see it now. Hampton coming here - the man in the money suit that Dorothy mentioned - coming to this seedy Village bar to try one last time to bring his little girl home. But Cherry didn't want to go, did she Doug? You knew she wouldn't, knew you couldn't convince her, you'd tried so many times. So you did the only thing you could think of. You tried to have her committed.

But if Hampton did that, then why hire me to find her? He signed the form, he handed her over to Omega. How could he not know where she went? Unless...unless...

Omega didn't tell him.

Hampton would have huffed and puffed but, even as rich as he is, the house of Omega wouldn't have blown down. That's why he hired a PI. Omega must have had Hampton by the balls somehow, but a dick is free to poke its head in anywhere. Omega took his little girl and didn't tell him where.

Why? Seems to be the most pertinent question lately.

I reach my Chevy, juggle the keys into the lock. I punch in Kastle's number on the cell phone. The phone rings, rings. Come on, come on. Where is she?

Kastle finally picks up. Sounds like she's at a bull fight. Can barely hear her but I manage to yell a question about Omega down the phone.

"They're a global pharmaceutical corporation," she says. "Been in the news because their stock's been plummeting all week, some other big wig corporation is trying to buy them out. Trask, the CEO, sold all his shares just before he died and the rest of the major stakeholders have followed suit. The rats are abandoning the sinking ship."

"Ever heard of the Omega Institute? I think it's a hospital."

"They're all over the place, one in the city, three upstate. Private hospitals for the rich and famous. Lindsay Lohan does her rehab through them, she can't stay off the formalin apparently. Heard a rumour Omega were going to buy the old state psycho hospital on Randall-Ward Island. Could never confirm it though."

"What's Hob got to do with Omega?"

"Not sure," Kastle says. "Heard he was a shareholder, that's all I know. Why? What have you found?"

"You'll get it all, Kastle, I promise." Looking around the empty street I can't help but laugh. "Hey - why is it so quiet, if there's so much shit going down?"

"God, Jonny, turn on your radio. There's a curfew, the cops are trying to quell the violence. I'm at the Rockefeller Centre and it's not working. People are tearing each other apart here...ooting and, Terry, Terry you see that? Jes...yeah, go, g....araday, I have to call you ba..." The signal cuts out. If Kastle doesn't watch herself she'll be the one who's torn apart. I'm not worried about her, though. She can take care of herself.

I click the phone shut and head for 5th Avenue. I have some questions for Douglas Hampton III.

Except for the two ambulances screaming south and a blaring cop car running on a parallel street to me, the streets are a ghost town. Shops are dark, the pavements empty. A breeze rustles the trees bordering Central Park and there are flitting shadows in the bushes. They say hundreds of homeless Newly Dead gather in the Ramble when the park closes at 1am, now that the city changed the trespassing law to allow them space to gather. I'd hate to be in the park tonight.

The lobby of the Dakota Building is a blaze of lights and the doorman's missing in action. Can almost imagine tumbleweed tumbling by - as long as it's diamond studded tumbleweed, that is. I take the elevator to the penthouse, *Girl from Ipanema* muzak oddly comforting during the ride up. The hallway to Hampton's apartment is empty. And the door's open.

Inside, dark. My shoes tap too loudly on the polished wood floors - why is everyone else's apartment better than mine? - but I don't have to walk far to find him lit by an overturned lamp in the lounge. Douglas Hampton III. At least what's left of him. A pile of goo and ash in the lounge. I guess I can keep that retainer now.

The stench of chlorine is in the air and you don't need to be a PI to guess what's happened. The same thing that happened to Cyrus Beaumont. Someone's cleaning up their mess.

I put a call to Gannon. I don't want to but this is a crime scene and I think this disproves his suicide theory on Cherry. Really, I just want to see his face when he realizes I'm solving his case better than he ever could. Or maybe there's a part of me that wishes we were working the case together, like the old days. Or maybe I just want to rub it in.

The phone rings and rings, then clicks to his message bank. "Just thought you might be interested in solving the Cherry Hampton case," I say into the phone. "There's a really big clue at Douglas Hampton's place, if you can be bothered to go and find it." I give him the address and click the phone shut.

Then a voice: "Look what we have here, Dutch."

"Indeed."

I turn and come face to face with the mixed life twins. They look so much bigger when they're blocking the exit. I contemplate putting up a fight, but against guys this size it's better to let them think they have the upper hand.

The dead one – is it Butch or Dutch? does it even matter? – raises his fist. I've done this dance before.

"Not the face," I plead.

He punches me in the face. Asshole.

The world is watery.

Goes black.

I come to at one point, hearing Gannon's voice through a ringing haze. There's a dead hand over my mouth, my arms locked behind my back. I can't move, can't talk. The Arnie twin's hand smells like a decomposed cow would after a dip in the pool at the local Y. Chlorine. They've been having fun with acid again.

We're in a bedroom, a big one to accommodate me and the Arnie knockoffs. I can see Gannon through the partially open door. He's kneeling over the pile that at one time was Douglas Hampton III. I struggle but find I can't move in the slightest, jammed between the sides of beef.

Butch whispers to his cufflink: "Another gentleman has arrived. A cop." He taps his earpiece radio, waiting for a reply. I want to pull at the cord hanging from his ear, find out who's on the other end of the line, who the puppeteer is that's holding the strings of these big fucking puppets.

Butch nods as he listens. Then he says: "Indeed."

Gannon's talking on his phone, calling it in, and then it hits me. I led him here. The only reason Gannon found Hampton was the phone call from me.

And then I see Butch raise my gun, the Beretta they took off me outside the Closet Skelton the first time they kicked my ass. He aims at Gannon's back.

I whimper against the dead fingers.

"Back to sleep, little man," the necro brother whispers, squeezing his hand.

My air is gone, everything goes black again.

But I hear the gunshot.

A shot...

*I'm in a bar in Tribeca, dirty, dark, the entrance in a
stinking alleyway full of wandering dead. I'm moving too
quickly to be walking, I have no control of this dream/memory, I
can't stop myself. I go through the doorway and the muted neon
stripes the faces of the young prostitutes at the bar. They look
dead, deader than they really are, years of turning tricks for
necrophiliacs wearing down their souls. Dead girls don't need to
eat or sleep like live ones, they don't carry disease, and nine out of
ten men can't tell the difference between them and a living girl
anyway.*

*There's a hallway ahead, leading to the back and the
screaming that brought me inside the bar. I head for it because
hat's what I do, what cops do, they try to stop the screaming they
hear.*

*The cries lead me to a room, a room with two people
inside, a room I don't want to see into but I can't stop myself, this
is a dream and dreams don't stop easily. Nor do memories.*

*In the room there's a girl. She looks just like Cherry
would if she'd been fucked too many times. She's tied to a bed
and she's crying, crying so hard I want to kill her myself to stop
the wailing, the way it scratches at my mind. She looks dead
already. But she's not. Not yet.*

Gray Gary J.

*Gray Gary J is putting something in the girl's arm, a
needle, and in the dream it's as big as he is and written up the
side are the words: UNKNOWN SUBSTANCE but I know
it's a speedball, an overdose, a mix of ice and formaldehyde and
God knows what fucking else. Pimps give it to girls to kill them,
so that when they relive their heads are messed up. Makes them
undead junkies in a trance they never break out of. Makes them
easy to control. Easy to fuck over and over again.*

*Gray Gary J has a shit-eating grin on his face and an
erection strains his leather pants. He's enjoying this.*

*The girl – I don't know her name, I never knew her
name, she's everygirl to me – the girl's dreams slowly die.*

He's killing her and I'm watching. I have to save her.

But then she looks at that fucking smile on Gray Gary J's fucking face, and she fucking says to him: "Thank you."

And that's what makes me snap.

Just the thought of this girl, this living, breathing human being, thanking the man who's murdering her, who's making her into just another dead junkie whore on the streets of New York Fucking City, is enough to make me scream.

I can't take it anymore.

I can't.

I.

I lose it.

I charge Gray Gary J, slam him against the wall, start kicking the crap out of him, beating him for all the shit I've seen, all the calls I've come to where girls are killed for their undead ass, where dead men have been set alight by self righteous lifists, where little boys have been turned into zombie sex dolls for the perverse pleasures of pedophiles, where Newly Dead students have been strung up from the flagpoles as a joke, where a Dead African American woman sat in the wrong spot and was thrown from a moving bus, where good people, living people, have lost everything when they die and they step to the edge of the abyss and resolve to take a few people with them before they go.

I've seen it all and I don't want to see anymore and I kick and I kick and I kick Gray Gary J until he's nothing but a lump that used to be a person.

I hit him until he died.

I'm a murderer.

Chapter 16
The Big Sleep

I wake up.

White light, white walls.

The world's too bright, too clear, too pure.

I'm lying in a corner, naked.

Where am I?

I check myself. Don't feel anything.

I sniff. Nothing.

There's a mirror taking up a whole wall. I stand up, walk over. A pale face stares back at me. My eyes are black rimmed, bloodshot. I knock on the mirror. No answer.

No sound.

No noise at all.

Not even the sound of my own breathing.

Not...

Fuck. I'm not breathing.

I check my pulse.

No pulse.

I cup my hand to my mouth.

No breathe.

Fuck fuck fuck fuck fuck.

I'm dead.

Fuck.

Chapter 17
One Lonely Night

They say life makes more sense when you're dead. Death offers clarity. Of course, they also say death can drive you crazy.

I've seen the shows, read the papers, there are a lot of people out there who are fucked up because they died and relived. Something ends up firing wrong in their dead heads. They say being dead can really mess with your mind. I'm starting to see why.

It's not just the lack of a heartbeat, you know. I never really felt my blood pumping when I was alive, except on the odd occasion I had to take my own pulse, had a headache, felt my heart skip at the sight of a pretty pair of legs. It's not something you pay a lot of attention to. Never thought I'd miss it.

The senses go when you die. You can't smell anything, there's no taste. The air is just air. Not that you can tell anyway, because you don't breathe anymore. You're not cold, not hot, not anything. Numb.

You can still see, so I guess that's something to be thankful for. The only blind Newly Deads are those whose eyes were broken before they kicked. But the world looks different through dead eyes. Duller. Dull and numb. That's the only way to describe what I see now. What I am.

What really gets you when you're dead are the thoughts. See, Newly Dead are Newly Dead because the brain's still functioning. Scientists say the electrons are still firing, which is why the flesh relives since the synapses keep making everything moving. But those electrons do more than that. They keep the consciousness churning as well.

I don't know if it's because I just died or not, but all I can think about now is the fact that I'm dead. That's the thought that makes me shiver.

This is someone's fucked up idea of a joke, I just know it.

The light in the room comes from the ceiling; the whole thing's mottled like glass, shedding harsh light. The cell is six by six, the mirror takes up one wall. The door's adjacent the mirror, a thin seam, no handle.

What is this place?

I don't know how long I've been here, in this too white room. Feels like an eternity. Kastle told me time is different when you're dead. There's more of it to go around. More time to think. Looking at these fucking white walls, I'm not surprised. Never thought I'd long for the grey streets of the city. Never thought I'd want to hear the clarion call of taxi cabs. Never thought I'd miss the stench of millions of unwashed souls mingled with hotdogs from Gray's Papaya and pigeon shit.

Nostalgia rises like bile in my throat. This isn't me.

These thoughts aren't me.

I try to sleep. Can't. I once read an article that said the reason Newly Dead don't sleep has to do with that the state of being undead, which keeps the brain turning and turning and, if a dead person did sleep, that would mean the brain would shut down and they'd no longer be undead. Of course, another article I've seen said the reason necros don't sleep is because the devil is inside them. Don't believe everything you read.

Walking the white walls, not much else to do. I steer clear of the mirror. A while ago (how long? I don't know, could be minutes, could be hours) I looked into the mirror to see if I could tell how I'd died. No gunshot wounds, no stab wounds, not even needlepoint work up my arm or on my ass, nothing. I can still talk – I sing a few bars of *Star Spangled Banner* and I still know the words – so my larynx works. My skin's pale already and skin colour's the easiest way to spot a dead man, since without blood pumping there's no ruddy pink glow, nothing to keep the sallow out of the cheeks.

Finally I spot bruises on my neck and chin, just the right size to fit the palm of a necro as big as a pro-wrestler, and my throat's blue. Fucker choked me.

Not that there's a better way to die, but still. I always thought I'd either go in a hail of bullets or live to a ripe old age and die with a buxom young nurse giving me a 'special' sponge bath. To be choked by a couple of ex-wrestlers who talk like idiots is not how I'd pictured it.

There's nothing else to do so I sit in the corner. Think.

Where the hell am I, anyway?

I would have thought the Arnie twins would have just dumped me in an alleyway. Considering they shot Gannon with my gun after I called him to Hampton's apartment, you'd think the best course of action would be to let me loose on the streets and hope the cops take care of me. I may have been one once, but cops don't take kindly to cop killers, especially when they're PIs. I'm a second class citizen already and now that I'm dead it's going to be ten times worse. Dead and a cop killer, as far as they know.

They'd throw me in the lockup and come morning there'd be nothing left but ash, and the DA would dismiss the case and everyone would go on with their lives as if nothing had really happened at all. No one cares about a dead man who doesn't come home. If anything, they'd probably think they're doing the world a favor by getting rid of another walking corpse taking up space.

As you can tell, being Newly Dead is getting me down. Just what the world needs – another depressed zombie.

When I was younger, my grandfather would tell me to always look on the bright side of life. He never said anything about there being a bright side to death. Then again, he also used to tell me the moon was made of cheese and America would be a better place if Bush Jnr was still president. Don't believe everything you hear.

Boredom sets in. I contemplate biting a couple of my fingers off and watching them race. The idea makes me even more depressed.

I start to think this is all part of *their* plan, whoever *they* are. Killing me, keeping me here. Ha, ha, let's lock up Faraday and watch him squirm for eternity. Ha fucking ha. At least they could have left me a pair of pants.

Retracing the steps that led me here, I try to think how I could have done better. Nothing comes to mind easily. One benefit of living without conscience. People say I'm an asshole because I'm like that. They're just jealous. They'd live like this if they could. Then I remember I'm dead and maybe a conscience isn't the only thing I should be missing right now.

I put my face up against the mirror, cup my hands. Impenetrable. All I see are my eyes turning white at the edges, my skin graying. Knock knock. No answer.

I spend some time looking at my fingernails. They keep growing when you're a necro, just like your hair, only the nails crack easier, wear down. Decompose. Dead women from the Upper West Side spend thousands on their nails; it's like a Newly Dead status symbol to have youthful nails to go along with your bottox detox or your new plastination job. I've never really noticed my nails before now. I should get a manicure.

If this is what you think about when you're dead, I'd rather be like Cherry.

Cherry, Cherry, Cherry. Why couldn't you have turned up in a hotel room in Chinatown, hung over, maybe a little beat up, probably infected with an STD that you could take a cream for, but still alive and kicking? Why'd you have to be the first American to not relive? And why did you have to land in my lap?

I pace. Ever tried pacing in a small room? The attraction wears off quickly.

Butch and Dutch, Butch and Dutch. Who are they working for? Someone who wanted Cyrus Beaumont dead, obviously. But I saw them before the Closet Skeleton, they were at the park where Cherry was found. Then they turn up in Hampton's apartment with their little bag of acid tricks. My cop instinct tells me they're independent contractors. A pair of toughs like that would be known if they were muscle for a local mobster. They never would have shown their faces at Cherry's crime scene if they weren't from out of town. So who's giving them orders?

When you're dead, you realize the only thing your body's going to do from now on is rot. Gives new meaning to the term middle age spread.

How long can this go on? I bet they've done research into how to fuck with Newly Dead and that's why nothing's changed in hours. Or is it days?

I curl up in the corner, put my arms over my face. That shuts out the light just enough for it to feel like I'm sleeping. Daydreams are the only ones you can have when you're Newly Dead. Mixed images. No rest. No rest for the wicked.

I think about my Indian landlord's daughter and the story she told about the dead people just floating away on the Ganges. Then I remember Kastle talking about the necros swimming off Carl Schulz Park, hoping the spot where the Harlem and East Rivers meet will somehow wash away their sins. I could do with some of that right now.

Screaming at the mirror doesn't make anything happen. I do it anyway. Makes me feel good. At least I have that. They say dead people don't feel anything. Fuck them.

Numb.

Numb.

I slam my fist into the mirror but it doesn't break. Nothing I hit breaks in here. Not the walls, not the floor, not the neccer face looking back me wildly.

I've been in here for days and they're going to keep me here for years, for the rest of my afterlife. This room is my coffin. My tomb.

When you're alive, you only ever want what you can't have. That's the nature of desire – the moment you attain

what you desire, you no longer desire it. Life's like that.
That's why life only makes sense when you're dead.
Because you can't have it anymore. And not being able to
have life makes you realize just how important it really is.
This is my afterlife.

I. Am. Dead.

Chapter 18
Blackmailers Don't
Shoot

Then, after an eternity, a voice: "Ah, Mr Faraday. Cozy?"

For a moment I think the voice isn't real – for the last two hours I'd been having an imaginary conversation with my old Uncle Bob, who used to live in Iowa before he relived and moved to Alaska for the cold – but then I recognize who the voice belongs to. Motherfucker. I had a feeling he was behind this.

Grandpa Hob.

A light comes on behind the mirrored wall with a flicker. There's a console, some chairs – your typical observation room. A Chinese man in a white coat is ticking a clipboard. At the back of the room, looming like stray pieces of Stonehenge, are the Arnie twins. I swear I can hear the dead one crack his knuckles from here.

And there's Grandpa Hob. That crusty old motherfucker.

"I trust the accommodation has been to your liking," he smirks. "I couldn't find you a smaller room, unfortunately."

My mouth's raw. "F-fuck you," I croak.

Hob sniffs. "As eloquent as ever, Mr Faraday. I believe you used to say the very same thing to me each time I walked out of your police station. I have to admit, it's rather tiresome after you hear it for the fourteenth time."

"H-how long have I been in here?"

The old zombie sneers. "Feels like forever, hmm? It's been a day, Mr Faraday, but time's different when you're dead, isn't it? There's a lot more of it. Now you know how I've felt for decades."

That, at least, gives me a good feeling. The thought that Ole Hob's spent years living like this.

I press on. He seems in a talkative mood. "Where am I?"

"Somewhere a lot safer than the city, I can assure you. Things are happening up there on my streets, Mr Faraday. New York is tearing itself apart."

I laugh. I sound like a ghoul. "They're not *your* streets, Hob."

The living Arnie says, "His mouth could do with a washing out, don't you think Butch?"

"Indeed. Shall we? It would be ever so fun."

Hob looks like he's contemplating it for a second before he waves the muscle away. "I think being dead is enough at this point. Besides, Dr Chan here wants Mr Faraday in one piece, especially after the last specimen I brought him was in a basket." Hob beams at the man in the white coat standing beside him.

Dr Chan. The hospital report on Cherry I found at the Skeleton mentioned a doctor named Xin Chan. He had admitted Cherry to the Omega Institute. The Chinese man behind the mirror smiles at me affably. Somehow his cheerfulness makes me shiver.

I can only imagine what Hob means by the term *specimen*. I want to keep him talking. "Who was the last...specimen."

Hob nods to Butch, who swivels a monitor on the console until it's facing me. On the screen is a closed circuit camera view of a room similar to this one, only the other room's got a table. Scattered on the table are body parts, pieces of clothing, a metal brace that once kept a dead head on a dead man. Linus. The busted z-boy who stutters like Elmer Fudd and fights like Daffy Duck. Linus is crispy from the train tracks and in pieces thanks to the A train. I may be a second-rate PI, but I do good work.

Linus's mouth is a gaping hole. He looks like he's hollering, spitting out words. Standing over him is Dr Chan and he has something in his hands but the camera view won't let me see.

"I've seen this one before," I say. "Check HBO. *Six Feet Under* might be on."

Ole Hob ignores me. "There's one thing my father taught me, Mr Faraday, before he went to the gas chamber for slicing up my mother," Grandpa Hob says. "He told me life is cheap. I saw that, growing up, coming up on the streets. Yet, I never really knew what he meant until I died."

On the screen, Dr Chan turns and he's holding a needle. Linus' thrashing intensifies. If it wasn't for the straps over his forehead and torso, he'd fall off the table. I can guess what's in the needle even if I don't know its name. The same unknown substance found in Cherry's body.

"But life isn't as cheap as it was in my daddy's day," Hob continues, his scarecrow hands tightening on the pommel of his walking stick. "The dead are cheaper than the living. Cheap, and plentiful. Like Linus here." Hob drums the monitor with a thin finger. "I found him in the Park sucking down ice, his neck as twisted as a dog's leg, offering his ass to any old fruit that wandered by. Just another neccer on the streets. One of the forgotten, the damned. I offered him a home, a purpose. A name. God only knows where he'd be without me."

I snort. "You're a real humanitarian, Hob. Expect a call from the Nobel Prize committee any day."

On the monitor, Dr Chan taps the needle, gives it an experimental squirt. The disassembled z-boy's eyes go wide. He knows what's in the needle, too.

"Oh no, Mr Faraday – the award shouldn't go to me. Dr Chan is the real humanitarian, and someday he will be recognized for the work he's been doing here at Omega. For now, though," and Hob puts a skeleton finger to his lips, "it's our little secret."

I don't want to watch the TV, don't want to see the doctor injecting the necro, so I ask, "What secret? I got to tell you, Hob, if you're trying to monologue like a villain in a James Bond movie, you're doing a half assed job of it. You've got me, I'm dead – ha ha, by the way – and I'm not going anywhere. Tell me what the fuck is going on." I find the best way to get someone to talk is to dare them. Bad guys love to tell you how clever they are.

Ole Hob takes the bait. "Always with the questions, aren't you? Very well, I shall...enlighten you.

"Dr Chan here has been working for some time on a number of, shall we say, experiments. As I'm sure you're aware, Newly Dead are notoriously hard to kill. To neutralize, I should say. You can hit us with just about anything and we keep on coming. Sure, burning works if it's hot enough, albeit slowly, and as Butch and Dutch can attest, a cocktail of acid and lit gasoline breaks down the flesh enough that a dead man doesn't get back up again. Not exactly cost effective or efficient, though. The problem is, and always has been, the Newly Dead brain."

On the monitor, Dr Chan injects the needle into Linus' nose. I start to think he's a bigger fruit than the first impression let on, until I realise he's sticking the needle into the z-boy's brain. You'd need a drill to go through the skull plate so the nose is the easiest option. Nothing but cartilage stopping you on your way to the frontal lobe.

Linus thrashes pointlessly, hurling abuse at the

doctor. Even with the sound muted the gist of the words are obvious. He ain't happy.

"Dr Chan is somewhat of a radical in his field," Hob continues. "He postulated that certain types of chemicals could induce unconsciousness in Newly Dead, possibly even a complete death. Given the right dose, of the right drug, the neural pathways would shut down, thereby effectively *killing* the undead brain."

Grandpa Hob laughs. It sounds like a death rattle deep in his throat. "As you can imagine, his work garnered some...*unfavorable* press, especially among the politically correct elite at Yale. It's funny, isn't it? The men who made a pariah of Dr Chan in public are the same ones who, in their spare time, swap their academic robes for black sheets so they can rape dead frat girls and feel good about themselves. But I suppose we all have something to hide, don't we, hmm?

"Like Linus. He tried to tell me the girl from Mr Beaumont's bar, the one who talked to you, Mr Faraday, was taken care of. I believed him. Charlie was in pieces and in no mood to talk, but I believed Linus. Why wouldn't I? Then I turn on the news and there's the same girl talking all about Ms Hampton to a reporter, and I just couldn't have it. Linus should never have hidden that from me. I'm his grandfather."

The camera zooms in on Linus' face. He's no longer screaming. He looks like he's trying to cry. He looks like he knows what's going to happen next.

"It took some time for Dr Chan to come up with the right...concoction," the crusty old bastard continues. "Don't get me wrong, the good doctor had some successes. One is a drug that puts the dead to sleep, which Omega will no doubt market as a relaxant. Another strain proved to be a highly potent and addictive narcotic, especially on the dead. I like that one so I'm taking it for myself. I'm calling it Reaper.

"There were many, many experiments, Mr
Faraday, and each one needed even more specimens.
That's where I came in. I'm Harlem's grandfather – all the
children come to me. Especially the dead ones, the lost
ones, the ones who had no purpose in life and their afterlife
is no better. At least here they're put to good use. At least
here they have the opportunity to be a part of something
bigger then themselves."

"So you sell your own kind as lab rats?" I ask.

The old necro's cracked face hardens. "Don't talk
to me about *my kind*, Mr Faraday. I was a black man before
I was a dead man and I've seen things done to my people
that an arrogant, over opinionated white man knows
nothing about, nor ever will.

"But I'm not bitter. America is, and always has
been, change. The only constant in this country is the fact
that nothing stays the same. That's all you can really
count on in America."

He's right, at least when I look at Linus. The z-
boy's changing, his dead eyes rolling back in his head, a
whitish foam gathering at the corners of his mouth.
There's a tic in his cheek and his tombstone teeth are
clenched. The dead aren't supposed to feel pain. Linus
looks like he is.

"Is that what happened to Cherry Hampton? Did
you sell her to Omega like the rest?"

Hob chuckles. "No, not I, Mr Faraday. It was her
father."

It's my turn to laugh. "You expect me to believe
that an Upper West Side yuppie would willingly give his
daughter to a deranged doctor and a dead gangster? You've
been smoking too much of your own shit."

"He would if she were dead."

Something clicks. The hospital form I found at
Cyrus' and the signature of Douglas Hampton III

I can picture him in his Armani, sick desperation

raising a sheen of sweat to his puffy face as he tries to convince his daughter to come home. I bet he couldn't believe the trash she was standing beside, some low-life bar owner with fresh tattoos and beer breath. That would have hurt Hampton more, the fact his apple-pie daughter chose someone like Cyrus Beaumont over him.

That must have been what his daughter had been crying about when she came back into the bar. What made her hide the hospital admittance form Hampton would have shoved in her face to convince her to come with him. He wanted her to go to a hospital, one of his hospitals, hoping it would bring her back to him, make her remember that she was daddy's little girl and she didn't need the drugs and the hooking.

But Hampton didn't know his daughter any more than Cherry knew her father. Maybe being told that she needed to go to a hospital – being told there was something wrong with her – made her do something she never should have done.

Dorothy hadn't said anything about Cherry being dead, and after that conversation, Dorothy hadn't seen Cherry again. Had Cherry finally given in to Cyrus that night, just like that girl in Tribeca had to Gray Gary J? Dorothy the head said Cyrus preferred zombie lovin'. Could her father's trying to admit her to a hospital have been the final straw to push daddy's little rebellious girl into something she'd regret?

I can see Cyrus (and he looks just like shiteating Gray Gary J) using all his charisma to convince the sorority girl that she could be young and beautiful forever, and that all she has to do is give up the crappy life she'd been living to embrace her glorious afterlife.

Did you let him kill you, Cherry? And then, when you relived to find a bar tender fucking you, and when you realized that you couldn't taste anything, couldn't feel anything, and that you would be dead forever, did you run,

Cherry? Run home to daddy? And then what did daddy do?

Ole Hob must be reading my mind. "There are different kinds of evil, Mr Faraday. Many, many different kinds.

"The father didn't sign the daughter over to Omega for her own good, even if he said so. No. He wanted to send her to a place where he thought she could be helped. Could be turned back. Could be *normal* again." The old necro shakes his head and the motion's almost one of sadness. "Ignorance can be evil, Mr. Faraday. There's no such thing as normal in America, not anymore."

Linus is dying on the screen and it's the most horrific thing I've ever seen and I can't look away no matter how much I want to.

"But it's not all bad. Cherry became very important to Dr Chan's program," Hob says, raising an eyebrow at the doctor beside him, "didn't she?"

Dr Chan nods vigorously. "Very important, yes." I can hear the Yale in his voice. "The patient in question was the first test subject to be injected with strain-67. Her response was...delightful."

The doctor goes back to scanning his clipboard. Hob grasps his shoulder like a proud father would a dutiful son. "He's a man after my own heart, hmm? And they say only the dead laugh at death anymore. Suffice to say, Mr Faraday, little Cherry was so important to us that when Mr. Hampton enquired about his daughter certain measures had to be taken. Enter Dutch and Butch, Omega's employees of the month. Not the most...inconspicuous when it comes to getting the job done, but they do get it done."

"Thank you," Butch says.
"Indeed," Dutch says.
"They cleaned up the trail. They took care of Mr Beaumont, Mr Hampton, even your ex-partner, Mr

Gannon, though I thought it was a nice touch when they pinned his murder on you."

"Indeed," Butch says.

"Thank you," Dutch says.

"And they took care of *you*, Mr Faraday. Your ex-partner has relived by now and will have found your gun, a bullet from which just happens to be lodged in his heart. Your name will be even less than what it is now. A former policeman who shot his partner in the back. You're a cop killer, Mr Faraday. Now *you* are one of the damned."

Linus is dying. It's tough to watch, just as confronting as watching a living person kick it and I've seen my share. Froth bubbles from his mouth, brackish and gritty with his insides. The muscles in his neck are stretched tight, too tight. He's bitten off his tongue and it's flopped onto his chin, lying there like a dead slug.

Linus shudders, spits froth.

Then he lays still.

Grandpa Hob is grinning like a skull. "See, Mr Faraday? Effective, and efficient."

I want to throw up but I'm not going to give him the satisfaction. "So why, Hob? I would have thought the last thing a zombie would want is for someone to find a way to put him in the ground for good. Seems like too big of an idea for a gangster from Harlem who runs girls and formalin smack."

"That's always been your problem, Mr Faraday," he gloats. "You think too small. Prostitution, racketeering, trafficking – that's small potatoes, compared to what Omega do. Try global pharmaceuticals. Did you know two thirds of the developed world reaches for an Omega product when they have a headache? The first world stave off everything from AIDS to MS and pay more than twice their weekly wage for Omega's miracle pills, when the cost of producing the drugs equates to a dollar a packet. Criminal, and very, very profitable.

"But it doesn't stop there. Try biological and chemical military arms, weapons that inspire revolutions and topple governments. Do you have any idea of the applications for strain-67? The world's soldiers are all Newly Dead, Mr Faraday, which makes it notoriously difficult to win wars. Takes a lot of firepower. Can you imagine strain-67 used as a weapon? Every country that wants to stay in the race will pay, and pay well. You call me a gangster, Mr Faraday? I am a saint compared to Omega."

"Are you in charge of Omega?"

The old necro waves a liver spotted hand. He's not in charge. And he doesn't like it either. "More of a subcontractor with stock options. I'm only here because I wanted to see *you*, Mr Faraday. I have been looking forward to this moment for a very long time."

He hasn't turned the monitor around. The screen's paused on Linus' dead, dead face. He's the second person I've seen, living or dead, lie that still. This must have been what it was like, back before we all became necros. The dead would be still. So, so still.

Being bold helps mask my fear. "Oh yeah. What moment is that, Hob? You've already killed me, so there's not much that frightens me now. Are you going to inject me, too?"

"Yes, but not with strain-67. Dr Chan here is going to give you a shot of Reaper. You'll get higher than you've ever been and then we're going to let you loose on the streets and watch you get torn apart by a life supremacist mob. At my personal request, of course. That should make for a fun evening's entertainment. Dinner and a show."

Fuck. Grandpa Hob is just the sort of twisted fuck to do exactly that. I may be in trouble.

Dutch and Butch turn to leave the observation room, following Dr Chan. They're all coming in. I long for the hours I was in here alone, then push the thought away. Stay sharp, Faraday. It could save your afterlife.

The mirror clouds over, I'm back looking at the neccer that I now am. Yeah? Well this neccer can fight. You'll have to stick me good, Hob.

The light in the ceiling pulses and suddenly I'm a lump on the ground, my arms and legs unwilling to move. I can't close my eyes, they're wide open, and it's like the light is flickering in my brain.

Flashing lights, the only way to stop a necro. Flashing light to a dead man like an anime cartoon to an epileptic. The only difference is necros don't go into a fit. We just can't move, the light pinches something shut in our brains. The motor neuron system says, *Fuck this, I'm outta here*, and you become a pile of dead limbs on the floor.

A seam in the wall of my cell splits, a door slides open.

Dr Chan and the living Arnie twin walk in. The good doctor has a needle in his hand. His pearly white smile is too bright.

Unfortunately I can still hear Hob's voice: "I hope you're not scared of needles, Mr Faraday." Then he laughs. Long and hard.

Motherfucker.

Chapter 19
survival...zero

God I feel good.

Being dead, I thought any kind of feeling was over, something I'd look back on with regret and a vague sense of missing something vitally important. But this drug, Reaper. Whoa.

The second the smiling lab coat injected me, the world wasn't the same. Even now, what must be five minutes of being dragged somewhere blindfolded and ten minutes of driving, my synapses are firing, shooting, blazing. My legs keep jerking, my eyes won't focus, my fingers snap of their own accord. It's like my body wants to dance and there's nothing I can do to stop that desire so I may as well go along with it. Not that I can right this moment, being tied up in the back of a van and all.

The van rocks as if we've gone over a speed bump. In the front are the Arnie twins, driving with apparent abandon. If I twist to look out the windscreen, I can just make out streetlights rushing by, rows of apartment building windows, the odd top of an odd tree. I really want to pay attention to what's out that windscreen yet my ambivalence is astonishing. I really, truly don't give a fuck.

At least they gave me my clothes back. I may not care what happens but I'd rather not have my dick swinging 'round if I can help it.

The engine vibrates through the floor of the van and the sensation of the metal pulsing against my cheek is like love.

Have you ever thought about the colour blue? No, I mean, really, truly, really thought about it? I have. I'm doing it right now. And I recommend it.

"Where should we drop our guest, Dutch?" one of the twins asks the other.

"The small gentleman said 110th and Amsterdam, Butch, at the Church of the Living Rosary."

"The *Living* Rosary? They would not like the gentleman in the back very much, would they, brother o' mine."

"Indeed. Methinks, not at all."

"Yes. Methinks it too."

I'm that stoned even the conversation of half wits has the ring of poetry. I try to get in on the act, try to ask the mixed life twins if we can stop for drive through 'cause I'd love a cheeseburger, but all that comes out of my mouth is a ghoulish moan. Makes me sound like the zombies do in those old monster movies. For some reason I find this hilarious.

Life never felt as good as the afterlife does right now. Grandpa Hob's going to make a fortune off this shit.

The living Arnie looks back over his shoulder. "I do believe the gentleman wishes to retort," he says. He waits a beat. "Well?"

I moan. I don't even know what I'm trying to say.

"I thought so. Eloquence, it seems, is not a prerequisite of the curriculum nowadays. A man like this seems, in my inestimable opinion – and you can disagree with me if you care to, Dutch."

The dead one inclines his head. "Noted. Continue."

"Very well. A man like this here, in the back, seems to have come from, how shall I say this? From the *very street* itself, to use, what?, a parlance-"

"Idiom? Colloquialism? Slang?"

"Indeed, one would find it to be all three, Dutch, if one were to use this gentleman as an example. In fact, one wonders, Dutch, if the gentleman here shouldn't be rejoining the street that he has come from."

The big 'un climbs over the seat into the back, a sudden, ominous shadow over me. Butch is bigger than Everest.

The ropes are tight. I could probably get a hand free if I could stop getting turned on by how it feels around my wrists. Shit. Did I just think that...or say it?

Butch says, "Ah, now methinks I know how your mind is working, brother."

"How so?"

"You think to expedite the gentleman's departure from said vehicle forthwith?"

"Indeed."

Rough hands grab my shoulders, hoist me against the side of the van. I think I have an erection but my neck isn't working well enough for me to be able to look down and see. Damn this Reaper.

"What do you suggest?"

"Merely that we act according to the small gentleman's wishes and, as soon as humanly possible, make tracks for the comforting confines of Omega

I laugh. Their conversation is the funniest thing I've heard since the time Conroy had to explain what that dead hand was doing down his pants. Slipped off the desk, my ass.

The dead twin sighs. It sounds like the last breath of a dying man. "I believe the gentleman was laughing at you. We don't like being laughed at, do we brother?"

The living twin looks me dead in the eye. When I blink, he becomes two. When I blink again, there's four, eight, sixteen of the fuckers staring at me and holding the collar of my shirt tight. And they're all smiling, too. Sixteen feet kick the doors of the van open. Cold wind whips me.

"Indeed we don't," the sixteen Butches say.

Then I'm flying.

The Reaper drug makes the fall last forever. Like floating in deep space, falling through water. Like the world's just a dream and I'm the dreamer. Like any moment I will land peacefully and safely. Or bounce.

I hit the tarmac, rolling, scrapping, as my body tumbles. My skull grates against the ground, a horrible, buzzing noise coming in short bursts like a migraine that comes, then goes, only to come and go again. I wonder what dead bits might be falling off me. Something snaps, must be my shoulder because the ropes loosen, the same shoulder that hasn't been the same since the A train.

Finally I hit a trash bin and stop. The aptness makes me chuckle.

The Arnie twin waves to me from the back of the truck as it speeds away, swerving to avoid a taxi. I want to wave back but my arm isn't working. Would you look at that? My arm's at a right angle to my body. How'd that happen? Oh, that's right. I'm dead.

I think I'm somewhere in Upper Midtown, it has that look. Lots of people in a hurry to go nowhere. Daytime, God only knows if it's morning or afternoon. There's a sign on a building that reads ERMENEGILDO ZEGNA and I think I'm going insane until I remember they sell clothes I can never afford.

A black Lincoln rolls past, playing *Lowrider* way too loud. People walk beside, over, around me, but no one's really looking, no one sees. Is it because I'm dead? Or because I'm sprawled against a trash can, looking like just another homeless necro bum on the streets of the Apple? This Reaper's taking a turn for the worse. I hate it when drugs make me think about myself. It's never good.

At least there's no pain when I pop my shoulder back in.

I put my head in my hands for a while. Try to steady myself. Doesn't work.

The pavement beneath my butt is a pebbly grey and if I look at it for too long I can see myself in its roughness, its coarseness, the very nature of it, and if I keep looking, if I look too much, I'm a part of the pavement, of the ground, of the gutter, of the whole damn shit-eating city, the entire godforsaken excuse of a fucking country that I call home, and shit – it really ain't that bad to be a part of it at all.

The Reaper makes you philosophical, too. Grandpa Hob's definitely on a winner with this drug.

I pick myself up. Literally. It's easier to do when you're dead. My left leg's off kilter but a rap from my fist as I walk and my knee clicks back into place. Some nasty gravel rash up my right arm, a little on the back of my head. I think about checking how I look in the mirrored window of a hotel I pass but a sneer of disgust from a woman who's a dead ringer for Ivana Trump's corpse makes me not bother. If I look that bad to a dead woman, lord knows what the living think of me.

Questions. I remember having a lot of questions, yet they, and their answers, are meaningless at the moment.

Heading vaguely south, down Fifth Avenue. I don't know why. Like most decisions I make under the influence of drugs, I try not to think about them too much.

The Reaper's thrumming in my head, a lovely buzz. This drug will go far if it makes a necro feel something. In fact, it almost feels like I'm breathing fresh air but the thought that I'm not breathing at all, and never will again, depresses me. Olympic Tower passes, the monolithic building resembling a giant's smooth sided Lego block, and the momentary darkness in its shadow suits my mood.

But then I'm in the sun again and there's St

Patrick's and there's a large group of people dressed in black sheets coming out of the cathedral. Life Supremacists. I'm fucked now.

The leader – you can always tell who's in charge by the size of his hood – is flanked by about two dozen more sheet-clad delusional assholes of various shapes and sizes. Lifers are like that. You could be living down the hall from one for all you know, you just can't pick 'em. At least not until they put a black sheet on once a month and crucify one of the shambling Newly Deads, some dead guy so old and broken down he can't defend himself. Kastle told me once the Lifers in Utah do whole necro families. Burn them on crosses to watch them wiggle. Even the children.

The Lifers are herding out the worshippers, mostly old women and dead tourists. One Lifer big enough to give Butch and Dutch a run for their money has an old priest by the collar, hoisting him high. The priest is a living man with one foot in the grave. Easy target for a bunch of fanatics.

"Knights of the Black Kamela!" the lifist leader proclaims, "I hereby declare this church, and all who worship within its walls, an affront to God Himself. It's time we cleansed it from the world. Life is for the living!"

"LIFE FOR THE LIVING!" the mob hollers back. I'm surprised they don't have pitchforks and flaming torches. Mind you, the crow bars, two-by-fours and tire irons look mean enough.

The Lifers keep the closest passersby away, and in typical New York fashion there's so many people still going about their business that what's happening on the church steps could just be another performance art piece by a bunch of film school wannabes. In bad taste, sure, but ultimately not as important as catching the D Train on time or deciding whether or not to have another mocha before lunch.

The old reverend struggles against the big Lifer's grip. "Please! Please...for the love of God..."

"You wish to sermon the dead? You think the word of God is for them?" the leader asks. His disgust makes him spit. "God doesn't care about the dead. That's why the dead walk amongst us. Sin. For their sins, God has denied them entry to paradise. We must burn for our sins, not deny them. That is the path to righteousness, Reverend O'Reilly. There are abominations walking this earth that must be sent to hell! Burn them to HELL!"

"BURN IN HELL!" the Lifers shout.

"...Tommy...that's...you're little Tommy Reardon, aren't you?...I know it's you...Tommy..."

The leader slaps the priest across the face. "You don't know me, old man. I'm not little anymore." He turns to the mob at his back, gives them a signal. "Let's see how God will judge this man!"

"JUDGEMENT!"

The Lifers are getting to me – there's only so much echolalia I can take from murderous mobs – but the Reaper drug has decided I don't need my leg muscles and every step feels weird, gangly. Like my whole body's gone to sleep. The sharp spires of St Pat's still shadow my steps.

The leader cradles the old priest's chin in the palm of his hand. It's almost an affectionate embrace. Then his fingers tighten against the reverend's cheeks.

"I'm going to spare you the choice that so many others have wrongly made. You have sinned, Reverend James Patrick O'Reilly. You will burn for that. And we shall see if God opens His gates to you."

The big Lifer kicks the priest's legs out from under him and slams him against the pavement. There's a crack as the man's head hits the ground and he goes limp.

Another Lifer, dark skinned arms poking from beneath a black sheet, steps up with a jerry can and splashes liquid all over the priest. I don't need a sense of smell to know it's gas. What else would it be?

The priest doesn't move. Blood seeps from the back of his head.

Then the leader flicks open a Zippo and drops it.

The rush of flame finally stops the people on the street in their tracks. Those closest to the burning man reel back from the wave of heat and scolding flesh. No one knows what to do until the Lifers holler and throw themselves at the crowd. Someone screams and everyone starts running. Except me. All I can manage is to quicken my shamble.

The Life Supremacists are picking the dead out of the crowd. Three of them tackle a necro boy dressed like a Calvin Klein model, one of those Newly Dead middle class kids who finally have something to be depressed about. The lifers flail at him with doubled up lengths of chain.

A pair of Dead Korean businessmen run past holding their briefcases over their heads as a pack of Lifers pummel them with baseball bats.

Two of the mob is dragging a crying necro woman away, one Lifer already hitching up the waist of his black robe in anticipation.

Smoke engulfs the street as undead are splattered with gas and set alight.

A Newly Dead mother shields her living baby as a Lifer sprays an aerosol can at her and thumbs a lighter. She's engulfed in flame and her child screams and she screams and I scream along with her.

I'm in hell. And I'm one of the damned.

A black sheet spots me. He's around my size (I think it's a he, I can't tell for sure) and he's hefting a club made from a wooden table leg. I'm guessing he's not redecorating.

Being outside a church, I contemplate praying. But God will see right through that old trick.

Chapter 20
Too Many Have
Lived

The Lifer smashes the table leg into my chest. Ribs break and suddenly I'm looking at the sky, laid out flat on my back. It's a good thing I don't need to breathe anymore, my chest is sunken.

But the pleasant pulse of the Reaper is leaving me. I don't feel so good anymore. Typical. A good drug's never around when you need it. The come down's going to be a bitch. If I live to feel it.

The Lifer is gibbering as he hits me again and again and again with that goddamn table leg. There are sickening crunches as he smashes into legs, arms, my chest. He wants to break every bone before he burns me and there's nothing I can do but cradle my head in my hands. The Lifer laughs hysterically. At least someone's having fun.

Then: hope, as a shrill whistle cuts through the crowd.

The cavalry.

The Lifer with the club stops in his relentless pounding as a row of cops in riot gear goose-step through the smoke, helmeted, shielded and brandishing long batons. They're lined up like soldiers. Soldiers suited for war.

My attacker doesn't know what to do with himself. He looks to his leader, who stands forth, proudly holding aloft a Life Supremacist flag, a black cross on a red background. He looks pathetically small compared to the line of riot police. But his faith is obviously sustaining him.

"WE DO NOT RECOGNISE YOUR LAW!" the leader cries. "ONLY GOD WILL JUDGE US!"

The whistle sounds again and the cops step forward in unison. There's still pockets of fighting going on – a burly, Newly Dead construction worker is fending off a couple of Lifers near me – yet the sound of a hundred pairs of police boots marching as one seems the loudest I've ever heard. I know what's coming. I used to be on the other side of the shields.

Police wash over the Life Supremacists, a tide of navy blue that's so dark your eye could mistake it for the same black of the Lifer's sheets. Batons swing, crunching into guts, heads, kneecaps. It's typical Roman tactics – keep the line and hit anything that tries to break through. The Lifers are scattered about the street in small pockets. They don't stand a chance.

The Lifer on top of me finally gives me a break and runs into the fray. He's cut down by three nightsticks before he gets to utter any rhetoric. And I was just starting to like him, too.

I manage to sit up, wince at the sight of the twisted mess of my body. I've had worse days than this. But not by much.

Head pounding from the Reaper, the best thing to do is wait it out. The cops will be on me soon, and even the thought of being recognized, of being taken in on a bum rap for shooting Gannon, doesn't bother me. After what Ole Hob told me about Omega, I'm sure I could cut a deal, get Gannon to do some investigating for a change and find out the truth. Yep. Take me in, boys, for I have sinned.

But then the dead construction guy near me gets hit in the jaw by a police baton and it may not be such a good idea to sit on my ass. The Newly Dead guy goes down beneath a swarm of blue uniforms. The cops are hitting anyone to break it up, even the necros holding their own against the Lifers. It's a fucking free for all.

One of the cops hitting the dead guy stops the beating long enough to spit on the corpse. "Uppity neccer," he says.

New York's gonna burn, Kastle had said. I hate it when she's right.

A cop's running at me, stick held high. He's a weedy one, gangly, the riot vest and helmet almost comically large on his thin body. The standards have obviously slipped since I was last at the academy.

The cop trips on the outstretched leg of an unconscious man, takes a skipping step that causes his helmet to fall over his eyes, and hits the ground on his knees. It must hurt because he screams like a girl and pitches forward, ending up on his stomach right in front of me. The helmet rolls off his head – he didn't have the strap done up properly – and I get a look at his face.

Conroy.

I want to ask him what the hell he's doing here but my mouth still doesn't work. All I can do is groan at him.

The CSI with the zombie fetish groans back. "Wh...what...?" he gargles. We sound as bad as each other. His eyelids flicker open, focus on my face. "F-faraday? Is that you? Wh-what happened? Faraday – you're dead!"

I roll my eyes. Leave it to a pathologist to point out the obvious.

Conroy tries to sit up, gets tangled in his nightstick, and ends up back on the ground. He has more success the second time around.

He hunkers over me, grins. "I can't believe it – Jon

Faraday, dead. Gosh. A lot of people would be very happy to hear that. Not the least of which Detective Gannon. I heard you killed him and he's real pissed about it."

I stare daggers at him and he gulps.

"I mean, um, gee Faraday, what happened? How'd you die?"

I shake my head, manage to will my arm to tap my throat.

It takes him a second to work it out. "Can't talk, huh? All right, all right, come on. Can you walk? All right."

He hooks an arm under mine, hefts me up. My legs are working a little and I shuffle along, Conroy bearing me on his shoulder.

I recognize a few of the cops mopping up the mob. A couple even stop their beating long enough to look at me. Great. Word has spread.

Conroy steers me towards the open doors of St Patrick's and inside the cathedral. Behind us the cops are cleaning up the last of the Lifers, dousing the fiery corpses. I try not to look at the charred remains of Reverend O'Reilly, withering on the stairs of the church. He didn't burn hot enough. He'll be a blackened walking corpse now.

Is it the Reaper or the riot that makes the walls inside St Pat's look warped somehow, as if all the straight angles were converging on a spot way up on the ceiling? Diffuse sunlight leaves shadows at the peaks of arches, paints stripes of stained glass blue and red on the floor.

Conroy's half dragging, half carrying me. Other people shy away from us and shrink behind seats and columns. They've come in here to hide. Conroy's uniform is putting them off.

He lowers me onto a long pew. Tells me he's going to find a first aid kit. I laugh and it sounds like a cough. I don't need first aid. But Conroy runs off anyway.

For a long minute I lay there. Stare at the ceiling. Wish for unconsciousness, something I'll never get that again. It doesn't matter right now. I'll take numbness if that's all I have.

Conroy comes back with bandages, a needle and thread. I groan at him that I don't want it but he either doesn't understand or chooses not to. He sews up cuts on my leg and chest, puts a bandage around my head – "It won't heal, you know that, but you got a crack in your skull so this'll keep your brain inside until you get it fixed, with some ceramic or something." – and swabs the old blood away with water from a basin.

When he's done, he stands back, looks me over. "Not much of an improvement, I'm afraid, but it'll have to do." I hate not being able to speak. Conroy's scoring off me and I can't retort.

"...ug...," I manage to whisper. "...d...ug..."

Conroy frowns, and then his eyebrows shoot up. "Drug? Is that what you're trying to say? You're on some kind of drug?" I give him a tired nod. "What sort?" I give him a tired shake. "You don't know? You want me to take a sample? I should take a sample. I'll take a sample."

He uncaps a syringe from the first aid kit. "I really need to take some fluid from your brain, Faraday..."

Ugh. Just what I need, another needle in my fucking head. But if he has to, he has to. I moan and tip my head back. He plunges the needle into my nose.

"I know what you're thinking," Conroy says as he sucks at my brain. He's grinning. "What am I doing suited up? They called in everyone, Faraday, anyone with a badge, it's that bad. Most of us CSI guys did the first year of training at the academy so we're qualified, if you can believe it. I'm not a field man, you saw me out there! Couldn't even keep my helmet on. Boy. This morning I never thought I'd be in a riot."

You and me both, Francis.

"There," he says, stepping back. There's a mixture of blood and clear liquid in the needle. Why do I keep seeing my own blood? Conroy pops the cap back on the needle and puts it in his pocket.

The cathedral doors slam open. "Where is he?" someone shouts. "Faraday, you fucker! Come out here!"

Detective Ray Gannon clomps up the aisle, swinging his authority like a Louisville slugger. He looks like a bear whose honey's been stolen. And at the moment that honey is me.

He scowls when he catches sight of me. Conroy was right. He's pissed.

"Shit," Conroy hisses. "I, um, um, um, shit. I, you, um, I didn't know it was you, right? If he asks. Tell him that, Faraday, please." He reminds me of those kids you used to see in school that would fold at the first sign of authority. Fold like a sheet.

Conroy spins and faces Gannon. "I, um, apprehended the, um, perp, sir," he stutters, but Gannon ignores him, pushes past. Not even a *I'll deal with you later.* No, Conroy can relax. He just wants me.

The asshole pulls out his badge and throws it in my face.

"This is gonna make me so fucking happy," he spits. "Faraday – you're under arrest. Do me a favor and don't come quietly. Fucker."

Chapter 21
They Can Only Hang
You Once

It's a good thing I'm dead. Otherwise the beating
Detective Ray Gannon's handing out would probably kill
me.

He's been pounding for a good twenty minutes
now. He started with a baton, and then went to the busted
phone book he brought down to the morgue with him,
slamming the book against my face. I used to watch him
hitting a perp with that big old book. Always wondered
how it felt. Guess I know now.

He's mostly using his fists though, obviously
enjoying the meaty sound they make each time he connects
with my stomach, my kidneys, my jaw. You can tell he's
enjoying it. You couldn't wipe the smile off his face with a
nail gun.

I can only guess at what Gannon's fists are doing to
my insides. When you die, everything but your brain
shuts down. The rest of your bits and piece are
superfluous and have to be removed, otherwise they rot
away and add to the smell. Most Newly Dead get rid of
their organs as soon as they can after death, usually paying
a bit more to their embalmer to dispose of their heart,
stomach, lungs etcetera. I haven't had the chance to make
an appointment with my taxidermist yet, but from the way

Gannon's hammering away at me I won't be needing one. My ex-partner looks like he wants to put me in the ground for good.

The Reaper's worn off enough that talking's an option. But I have to spit out blood to get to my words. "...Ray...you've got to listen to me..."

He hits me in the face and a broken tooth bounces off the floor.

"You have the right to remain silent and refuse to answer questions, do you understand?" Gannon says.

He's been doing this the whole time, reciting the Miranda Rights. Like that gives him the right to beat on me. Or he knows how much I can't stand them and it's just torture for torture's sake. Either way it's fucking annoying.

Not for the first time since he threw me in here I wonder why no one's come in to stop this. Then it hits me: I'm a Dead American and a cop killer. No one's coming for me. That's why Gannon didn't book me, process me, take me to a proper interrogation room. The morgue's where you take the dead.

"I didn't shoot you!" I cry, which earns me another freight train slap. Luckily I'm handcuffed to the chair or I'd be on the ground.

Gannon chokes me with a baton, chokes my words. He says, "Anything you do say may be used against you in a court of law. You have the right to consult an attorney before speaking and to have an attorney present during questioning now or in the future. Understand, fucker?"

I manage to whisper, "...call...Brenda..." and the mention of my ex-wife's name makes Gannon loosen his grip. For a moment he might actually let me talk.

Then he grabs the nape of my neck and slams my forehead against the table once, twice, three times. Dark stars swim in my vision. Fuck. He could give me brain damage from this. Wouldn't that just top off the great week I've been having?

Gannon hisses in my ear, "Brenda's gone, Faraday. She left because she couldn't live with a dead man. I have you to thank for that." He crashes my head against the table again.

There's a ringing in my ears I'll never get rid of. "Listen! It wasn't me, Ray. I didn't kill you."

Gannon's only been dead a day and his skin's already graying. A pale hand throws something onto the examination table beside me. My gun, wrapped in a plastic evidence bag. "Found at the scene of *my* murder, Faraday. Your Beretta. How do you explain that?"

It's a perfect frame. Ole Hob knows what he's doing. He wouldn't call himself a mobster if he didn't.

That was the point of the crusty old sonofabitch's monologue back in the white room. He knew, no matter what he told me, I wouldn't be listened to. I'm a murder suspect in a police shooting. Even if I survived the Reaper and the streets, Hob knew the cops would put me in the darkest hole they could find and throw away the key. And I'd take all of the old neccer's dirty little secrets down with me.

"Think, Ray. Why would I shoot you? Sure, you're an asshole, but-"

I don't get to finish the sentence before he punches me again. Something trickles out of my nose – probably old blood – but it could be brain for all I know. It's worse being a zombie because you can't feel it. Your imagination's the only thing that works the way it used to.

"You're a killer, Faraday. I saw what you did to that guy at the Dakota. Rang me up to brag about it, huh? Same thing you did to that faggot Village bartender. You burned 'em all up. I found you at the scene. You named the fucking acid, Faraday. I knew I should have locked you away then, I knew you were lying. Hell, if the coroner hadn't ruled the girl's death a suicide, I could almost pin that one on you as well. I've got *your* prints on *your* gun and *your* bullet in my fucking heart, Faraday."

His smile is grotesque. The grin of a contented villain. "I fucking got you."

"Cherry didn't kill herself, Ray."

"Bullshit. You just can't accept it. I thought you'd be used to this after what happened in that bar five years ago. The Hampton girl's the same. Just another junkie bitch who thought death would be better than living. Guess she fucked up, huh? Of course, there was no pimp to beat to death this time, was there Faraday? No, you had to kill a cop this time."

His smugness makes me sick. "Listen, motherfuc-"

My own gun slams into the bridge of my nose, rocking my head back. When my eyes can focus I see black blood staining the plastic evidence bag in Gannon's hand. My blood.

"Do me a favor," Gannon says, raising the gun, "and fucking die."

He hits me again and again and again. Skull and gun connecting sounds like deep bass when you're Newly Dead. Thumps resounding in the depths of somewhere way down. Like a tolling bell.

Gannon looms over me. He's going to crack my skull. The Beretta is a sodden mess in his clenched hand, dark with blood and clots of my hair. It's hard to kill a dead man. But he's going to try.

Then: "Detective Gannon! Stop this!"

The pounding ends as Gannon, surprised, turns to the door. My left eye's still working and hopefully what I see means I do have brain damage. Twice in one night he's come to my rescue. I'm never going to live this down.

Conroy strides into the morgue. "You must stop this, Detective! Enough!"

He's trying to sound forceful but the roll of computer paper trailing from his hand gives the scene a certain ludicrousness. Like an IT nerd picking a fight with the varsity jock.

Gannon looks like he's about to turn on the CSI. Conroy suddenly realises he's confronting a necro twice the size of him and waves the paper at Gannon like a matador to a dead bull. "You have to see this, Detective. Results. Faraday's blood work."

My ex-partner scowls. "I didn't order any goddamn bl-"

"I ran a sample of his cerebrospinal fluid I took at the scene." Conroy's all twitchy as he lays the paper on the examination table, smoothes it out. "You're not going to believe this, Detective – I found another unknown substance."

"What? He's got the same stuff as the Hampton girl? Why is he still moving than?"

"No, it's not the same substance. But it's similar. Here, look at this." Conroy points at the paper. "This is what we found in Cheryl Hampton's bloodstream. And this, this is what I found in Faraday. See? Do you notice the similarities?"

Gannon shoots Conroy a dark stare. "I don't understand this shit, you know that."

The pathologist shakes his head, screws up the paper. "Look," Conroy says, desperate, "when I found Faraday, he was on something. I ran a test and nothing in our databases matches it, same as the substance in the Hampton girl that the FDA had no record of. They're not the same drug but molecularly very similar, with only minor alterations at certain points. What I mean is, whatever was injected into Faraday came from the same lab as the drug that was in Cheryl Hampton. In fact, judging from these results, I'd bet it was even made by the same chemist."

"Chan," I mumble, mouth gummy with blood. I spit a glob on the floor. "Xin Chan. Hob called him a scientist but neglected to add the 'mad' to the title."

"Hob? Grandpa Hob?" Gannon's curiosity and Conroy's bullshit has bought me what I needed. A chance to talk.

See, Gannon was never going to interrogate me. That's why we're talking in a morgue. No one asks questions in a morgue. But now that Gannon's appetite has been whet by the thought of getting some dirt on one of the city's most notorious gangsters, he can't help himself. He's a typical cop. He's just like me. He wants answers.

I tell him everything. I start with Dr Chan and his big fucking needle of Reaper, then onto Hob, and Omega, and the drug called strain-67 that sends Newly Dead to the big sleep. I tell Gannon about waking up dead in the white room, killed by the twin Omega bodyguards Hob used to dispose of Cyrus Beaumont and Hampton. Gannon must believe at least part of what I'm saying as he lets Conroy patch me up while I talk.

Then I get to the part where Gannon dies, shot by the mixed life twins while he crouched over the smoking corpse of Douglas Hampton III, and something steels in Gannon. He doesn't stop me when I mention the Arnie with my gun, but it's hard to know if he believes it.

I tell him they took my gun outside the Closet Skeleton when they beat the shit out of me. At least that gets a laugh from him.

"You never could fight, Faraday," Gannon says.

"Yeah, but I'm an even worse shot, remember?"

He doesn't say anything for a while. From years of being his partner, I know this is what he does when he's thinking. Goes all quiet. Motionless.

Conroy sews up a slash in my chest with black thread. He clicks my leg bones back into place. Tells me I need to see an embalmer right away and offers me the number of his cousin in Queens. I tell him I'll think about it.

Eventually Gannon speaks. "Okay." He stops, looks right at me. "Say I believe you. Where's the proof? I can't get a warrant for Hob based on your word. You ain't exactly a reliable witness, Faraday. Hopped up, fucked up, and with the history of bad blood between you and Hob, who'd believe me? Back in the day you arrested him how many times?"

"Fourteen."

"Yeah, right, and you never got it to stick once 'cause you never had any evidence."

He's right. Not even Gannon, as a fully fledged New York detective, could accuse Grandpa Hob of what he's done with only my testimony. Eye witness is not enough, Brenda used to say, you need the smoking gun. And the smoking gun, in this case, could only be found in one place. Omega.

"But where?" Gannon asks when I voice the idea. "You never said how you got in that white room or how they got you out, they drugged you, right? You could have been out for hours. They could have drove up from Washington for all we know. Omega's got offices in the city, a couple of hospitals across the river, not to mention hundreds across the country. Where do we start looking?" Being dead seems to have mellowed Gannon. Or maybe he's just exhausted from kicking my ass.

Hang on – the river. What was it about the river? Cherry was found where the Harlem and East meet. And if you head north up Harlem River, you get to...

It hits me. "An island. Randall-Ward's Island. Kastle said she heard Omega wanted to buy the old Manhattan Psychiatric Hospital on Randall-Ward's. And Randall-Ward's..."

"...is north of Carl Schurz Park, where Cheryl Hampton washed up." Gannon finishes the thought, doing that thing we used to do when we worked a case together.

He rubs his stubbly chin. "You think that could be the place?"

"White room, a doctor, crazy dead men – where else but an abandoned psychiatric hospital? I wouldn't bet my life on it but I'm dead anyway, so what the hell? Yeah, that could be the place."

Gannon sighs. He walks around behind me. He's still holding the Beretta in the blood soaked bag. He taps it against my shoulder as if in thought.

Then he leans down and whispers, "If you're lying to me, Faraday...I'm going to bury you."

There's a click as he undoes the handcuffs. He straightens up and tosses the gun in my lap. "Can you walk?"

I wave away Conroy's helping hand, struggle to my feet. My body feels rubbery, unsure. But I can stand and walk. I slip my Beretta from the plastic and ratchet a round into the chamber. Not out of the fight just yet.

"I took the tour once," Conroy says apropos of nothing. The CSI is packing away his medical kit, fastidiously slotting scalpels into sheaths, rolling bandage. "They do tours on Saturdays now. Manhattan Psychiatric has a cult following since the fire last year. The brochure said the tour would scare the beejezus out of me. I fell asleep. It was a walking tour. Do you know how boring a walking tour has to be to put you to sleep? Worst ten bucks I ever spent."

"You've been to Manhattan Psychiatric?" I ask.

"Oh yes."

"Then you're coming with us."

Conroy blanches. He turns paler than the two necros in the room. "But, but, but," he says.

"No buts."

"But I'm not a field man. I can't investigate an active case." His eyes nervously flick to Gannon. My ex-partner is stone. Conroy's moustache twitches like a scared mouse. "You saw me at the church. I'm useless."

I slap the pathologist on the back and he stumbles. "Nonsense. You're coming with us. Just...just think of the science, Francis. We need you to identify strain-67 so we can destroy it." I stare at Gannon. Is he on the same wavelength? "Right, Ray?"

Being dead makes you think differently. There is no way Omega's little experiments can hit the streets. In the wrong hands, in any hands, they'd be deadly. There's no law against killing necros. You can't be tried for killing a dead man, lawyers like my ex-wife Brenda Ballbreaker say time and again. Dead rights have been trying for years to change the laws but it takes time. Time we don't have.

Gannon's struggling with himself. I can always tell because his face screws up and he closes his eyes. Is he thinking like a cop, or like a Dead American? I'm hoping for the latter. But I know he's blue, through and through, and the idea of destroying evidence doesn't sit well with him. Even evidence that could bust his undead ass for good.

I don't take my eyes from him. I have to know we're on the same side.

Finally, he looks at me. His eyes are almost pure white now, the pupils ghostly. "All right. We destroy it." He's been dead a day longer than me. I remember my first day in that white fucking room. A day's a long time when you're undead. That must be what made up his mind.

"But I'm bringing Hob in," Gannon says. "His ass is mine."

I think about making a Dead Homosexual joke but now's not the time. Maybe later. "He's all yours. Let's go."

Conroy says, "But, but, but," and Gannon says, "No buts!" as he storms from the morgue. The pathologist trails after the cop, his pleading falling on deaf dead ears all the way to the car.

Chapter 22
The Curtain

Gannon guns the patrol car up the FDR. Harlem burns in the distance. Thick smoke billows from half a dozen blazes dotted across the borough, a heavy shroud blotting out the lights of the city.

Gannon's hunched over the wheel. The FDR is quiet. We're the only idiots driving towards the fires.

The patrol car passes over Carl Schulz Park and I think of the dead girl who washed up there. I'm coming, Cherry.

I thought Gannon would be chewing his toothpick but he surprises me when he lights a cigarette from a crumpled packet on the dash.

"Thought you quit," I say.

He huffs. "Can't kill me now."

He's got a good point so I light my own. In that moment it's like it's five years ago, Gannon driving, the two of us versus the dark, dirty world. A perp once told me the best way to see New York was from the back of a patrol car, since you never got caught in traffic. I don't know about that. From the front is pretty good, too.

Then I remember the times Gannon and I would pull up at crime scenes to find another kid turned Newly Dead by gangbangers, another old neccer burning in an alley for the change in his pockets, another fuck toy that used to be a living, breathing kid. And the city doesn't look that good no matter where you sit.

Gannon says rioting between the necros and the lifers has been particularly bad in Harlem. I'm not surprised. Harlem's full of Dead Americans. I wonder if Grandpa Hob knows what's going on in his part of town. Then I remember it's what he wanted, so he can turn a buck on his drugs. I may have said the old corpse was Gannon's to catch, but he better get to Hob first. I could do anything tonight.

We take Triborough Bridge onto Randall-Ward's Island.

The streets of Randall-Ward's are quiet as a grave. The city joined the two islands together with landfill some time in the last century (Conroy would know when but he's babbling in the backseat so I don't ask). Some people wish they'd dig it back out to separate the living on Randall and the dead on Ward, most of who clock in at the sewer treatment works that dominate half the island. Shit job if you ask me, but when you're a necro you can wade through a million litres of liquid crap without even wrinkling your nose, so why not? Pays better than McDonald's, too.

The only problem is the living who flock to the parks they built on the landfill, destitute, desperate lifers made redundant by dead rights and looking for someone to blame. Newly Dead people have been found swinging from trees in those parks, hanging there long enough to have their eyes pecked out by birds. Necros snapped in half and left to crawl, legless for help. Burnings. There was always someone burning at Randall's Island Park.

But tonight the park is silent, empty. At least the bits of it rolling past the car window. The Lifers must busy elsewhere tonight and the necros must be locked away. At least those who can get off the streets. There are enough fires in Harlem to believe there's at least one poor necro shuffling around New York, prime for a lifer beating.

Soon enough we pull up out front of what used to be New York's state psycho ward. A flimsy chain link fence surrounds the mammoth building that looks like an uneven stack of crates. In places the cream façade is pitched with black from the fire that shut it down last year. The lawn's overgrown, TRESPASSERS WILL BE PROSECUTED signs cover the fence, and boards are lashed to the lower windows of the old hospital. Broken glass glitters under the sodium security light near the front door.

"Charming, you say you went on a tour here, Conroy?"

The pathologist shivers beside me. "It looks different in the daytime."

Gannon's at the back of the patrol car, muscling out flak jackets, shotguns, even a fire axe, no doubt for the locks. Conroy puts another Kevlar jacket over the one he already has on. How did this guy pass basic training? Then again, he's not a walking bulletproof vest like me and Gannon, so I guess he can afford to be careful.

I take a Remington pump-action shotgun, some extra clips for my Beretta. My ex-partner twirls the axe as he slams the boot, walks to the fence. Just like old days.

"Electronic lock," Gannon says at the gate. "I don't see the city shelling out for something like that." He points to the top of the gatepost. "And look – security camera." There's the shadow of a lens, a red light flicking in the gloom. The camera's working. "They know we're here," Gannon says.

"Good. That means we don't have to be subtle."

I put my shotgun against the lock and pull the trigger. Hot shrapnel showers me as the lock explodes. I brush specks of seared plastic from my hands and push the gate open.

"You never could hit anything unless you were

close enough to kiss it," Gannon says.

"That should prove even more that I didn't shoot you, Ray. I'd never kiss you. I know where you've been."

He grunts, a hollow sound coming out of his dead mouth. He's about to say something else but he clams up. It's probably about Brenda. But both of us know tonight isn't about opening old wounds. It's about making new ones.

We slink up the path, broken glass crunching beneath our shoes.

By the time we reach the entrance Gannon's all business, gun out and ready, sidling up beside the entrance. I slip into old patterns, mirroring his moves, watching for his signals as he tries the door handle. It's not locked. Gannon puts his back against the wall.

Conroy's behind us, struggling to draw his gun from the shoulder holster I strapped him in earlier. Should have put it on his belt. "Just stay back," I hiss.

Gannon nods to me. I cover him as he opens the doors and slips in. I follow.

Darkness. My shoes crunch glass inside. Gannon tosses me a flashlight. The light cuts across a ruined foyer. A half a dozen exits, two sets of stairs, too many closed doors that could lead anywhere.

I don't remember this place even if I have been here before. Still, the last time I was here I died and got off my face on Reaper. No wonder my memory's patchy.

"Which way?" I ask Conroy.

He shrugs. "It depends. Where do you want to go?"

I want to hit Conroy but I'm afraid he'll break. Through gritted teeth I say, "Just take us where the tour went. The front door was unlocked, Francis. That means the bad guys came this way. Show us around and we just might find them before they find us."

The CSI takes the lead and, to try and take his

mind off it, I ask him what happened at the hospital.

Manhattan Psychiatric, Conroy explains, used to be just your regular, run-of-the-mill psycho ward, a place to keep the crazies away from the rest of the city. But in a Newly Dead world, a different type of crazy was born.

A lot of people didn't relive to be as well adjusted as me and Gannon here. Some just plain snapped when they died – faced with eternity as a decomposing corpse will do that to you – while others relived with brain damage, came into their afterlife with ready-made-as-you-wait lobotomies. And because the government had a fair bit on its hands around then, what with their citizenry turning into zombies and all, the brain-fucked necros ended up clogging the mental asylums and hospitals across the country because no one knew what else to do with them. Asylums like Manhattan Psychiatric, which took in thousands of dead crazies for years after the Reliving. Until last year, that is.

"They don't know who started it first," Conroy says as he leads us down a hallway. The rooms off the hall are blackened pits of ash. "The Newly Dead patients or the living. A lot of people blamed the dead, of course. They outnumbered the living patients and staff two to one by that time. They're an easy scapegoat. But no one knows for sure."

"I heard it was over a game o' cards," Gannon says, ducking to look into a room, his gun up. Over his shoulder I see a twisted bed frame, dark with soot.

"It was in a rec room upstairs, if I remember right. The tour didn't mention it starting over a game of cards but by the end it didn't matter. The orderlies couldn't control the fight once it started, and by the time security got there they couldn't tell who was dead and who was living. Just a mob. Security shot into the crowd. Bullets don't stop dead people. They just make more of them. Soon enough one of the patients got their hands on the

guard's keys and...well, you can guess what happened
next."

I can see it as if it were happening right in front of
us. Wild eyed, slobbering necros tearing into nurses,
doctors, orderlies. The pristine white of the hospital walls
slathered with the red of blood. Mad undead taking out
their unimaginable torment on whoever crossed their path.
Monsters, like the monsters of old.

"The fire started in the boiler room and spread from
the ground up," Conroy says.   By the time the fire trucks
got here, the bottom floors were gutted and the crews
couldn't get in to rescue anyone.

"The fire burned so bright only a few of the people
managed to jump from the windows. The lucky ones were
caught in the flames while the ones who relived were
horribly scarred. The tour guide said most of the survivors
ended up in an asylum in Maine. Hundreds were burnt up.

"The government's still deciding what to do with
the hospital, though the tour guide did say the money
raised from the tour was going to a dead rights lobby group
who want to put a memorial here." Conroy sniffs. "All in
all, it was a boring tour."

The hospital is a maze. Hallways upon hallways,
rooms desolate and ruined. In places the paint's bubbled
from the fire, like burst boils. In one room the entire
ceiling has fallen through and you can see the floor above
through seared rafters like the broken ribs of a charbroiled
animal. In one room our shoes slip on the remains of a
couch melted to the linoleum. A television sits in a metal
cage above a doorway, the screen a slag of glass suspended
from the bars. Conroy takes us through a cafeteria. Ash
covers tables, chairs. The floor is scorched with stains that
were once people. This place gives me the creeps.

"Are you thinking what I'm thinking?" Gannon
asks me.

"Christ, I hope not."

"No, I mean where are all the guards? If the camera out front is working, why haven't we heard an alarm?"

The bull's right. I don't know what's worse – breaking into an abandoned psycho ward and being caught on camera, or breaking into an abandoned psycho ward and being caught on camera but no one is watching. Either this was a wild goose chase or the bad guys have already left. I was either stupid or late.

"Maybe we got past them," Conroy says. "Maybe we got lucky."

Maybe, but I'm not so sure. Luck's never been my lady, so why should she pay me a visit tonight?

We keep going and soon enough I'm wondering if luck hasn't totally taken a shit in my cereal bowl when Conroy stops us at an office. "This is as far as the tour went, we turned around from here," the pathologist says. He's apologetic but it's not his fault. Manhattan Psychiatric is a labyrinth. Like looking for a needle in a zombie stack.

"Down or up?" Gannon's getting impatient. He used to get a vein in his forehead when he was like this. Doesn't now he's dead, no blood to pump. He gestures to a set of stairs going either way.

"Down," I say. "Where else would an old corpse like Hob be?"

I'm trying to whet my ex-partner's appetite by mentioning the undead gangster and it works. Conroy clearly doesn't want to be here but a wave of the shotgun is enough to get him moving.

Gannon takes us down three flights of stairs before I tell him to stop at a door. He's puzzled until he notices the dim light under the door.

He opens it and we step into another hallway, this one lit by soft bulbs set in the walls. This hallway isn't covered in ash. It looks like someone cleaned house. Gannon and I exchange a glance. We're getting close.

Gannon stops at the corner of a T-intersection of hallways. He holds up a fist, wants us to wait. I hush Conroy. Gannon inches to the corner, looks around.

The muscles in his neck tighten and I ratchet my Remington, loading a shell. Gannon was right about my shooting ability. I'm not the best shot and the shotgun's my best chance in a gunfight.

But he relaxes, steps out. Whatever Gannon sees doesn't need shooting, so I drag Conroy with me around the corner.

There's a boy. A dead boy leaning his head against the wall, standing very still.

He's wearing a hospital robe done up wrong at the back, soiled Y-fronts over grey-white skin. He's looking up the hallway. He's not moving at all.

There's a bad vibe about this but that doesn't stop me touching the boy on the shoulder and turning him around. "Hey, kid."

The boy looks like a twelve-year-old Frankenstein. His eyes are dead, mouth open, tongue slack. A scar cuts his forehead almost in half, stitched up with thick, black string. Like someone got into his head. Literally.

I snap my fingers in his face once, twice. Nothing. I dismiss the irony of a mental patient losing his mind. Then I remember Cherry. She wasn't crazy, and she ended up down here, just like this kid.

"More of them," Gannon says at my back.

Further along the hall there are other dead children, some teenagers, others so young I have to clench my teeth from screaming. The hall looks like hell's own zombie playroom.

Chapter 23
The Killing Man

The Newly Dead children shamble and gape, gibber in corners, bang heads against walls. It's like being back in Manhattan Psychiatric's bad old days.

We pass rooms, doors wide open, and each one is a smaller version of the white room Hob put me in. A couple of Dead Puerto Rican boys, ten years old if they're a day, run when they see us. Gannon finds them huddled under a bed, unresponsive. A Dead African American girl draws mysterious black circles on a wall with chalk. Most of the children are vacant, empty. Lobotomized. Used by a twisted old neccer for twisted old ends. Fucker.

I add another bullet to Hob's tally. That's seven all up by my count. Six for Cherry and one for these lost souls.

"Why are they just walking around?" Conroy asks. He keeps trying to snap the little necros out of it, shaking them, talking to them. The ones who aren't missing their frontal lobes look so whacked out on Reaper or whatever the hell Omega fed them, that it's no use either way.

"That was why the front door was open, why no one's manning the camera," I say. "Looks like the experiment's over and they've let all the rats out. Hob's not going to the trouble of disposing of his evidence. He's going to let it walk right out the door. Just another lot of mind-fucked necros out there. Who'd believe a word they say? If you could even get a word out of one of them."

Just like a gangster to cut costs and let the streets take care of his garbage. *Everything comes to me*, Ole Hob had said behind that fucking sheet of two way glass while he had me trapped here, just like these kids. Yeah? Well karma's coming, Hob. Karma's a bitch. And I'm her boyfriend.

"I'm not gonna get a conviction on a bunch of deadhead kids," Gannon says. He's a good cop, true, but as subtle and heartfelt as a brick. "Where's my evidence?"

Conroy, surprisingly, takes the lead. Then I see the sign on the door at the end – LABORATORY – and it's clear why he's in front. Guys like Conroy can almost smell science. This is his Reaper.

The lab seems pretty standard to me – I've seen a few in my time and they all look the same – but you'd swear Conroy had sighted El Dorado. He gushes over this machine, lovingly touches that beaker, flicks through piles of notes that haphazardly litter the tables, *umming* and *ahhing* to himself like a man to a lover. The CSI has reached nirvana.

Gannon signals that he wants to move on but I make him stay. This whole thing feels like a fire sale, like Ole Hob has taken what he needs and cut himself loose and we're too late to pin it on him. Why else would they leave this shit just lying around? There must be something here we can use against him, some piece of evidence that can link the crusty old sonofabitch to the hell Omega created in Manhattan Psychiatric. Something...

"Anything?" I ask Conroy. This is his area of expertise after all.

The pathologist shakes his head. "If there were samples in this lab, they've taken them all. Nothing." He slaps a computer monitor as if it's a disobedient child. "The hard drives are gone and it'd take me weeks to go through these notes."

Fuck. "Keep looking, grab anything that looks relevant," I say to Conroy. "Ray – where does that other door go?"

"Looks like another corridor. There's a sign for a loading bay at the end."

Cherry's in my head. What happened to you, girl? Did you find a way to get free of Dr Chan? Did you run through here, did you see the mad works that had created the demon they injected in you? Did it mean anything to you or did you just keep running, looking for daylight, fresh air, the stars? Did you, Cherry?

"Oh, shit."

Not the reaction I was hoping for from Conroy – I was expecting more of a Eureka moment to be honest – but I can see why the pathologist chose those words. Beneath one of the tables, sitting there like a calling card from the Devil himself, is a bomb.

I've spent enough time looking over the shoulder of the bomb squad to know this one's a monster. The size, the shape. Enough C4 to blow a hole in the world. And a big fucking timer counting down from 5:00, 4:59, 4:58...

Hob wasn't letting the lab rats go. He was sending them all to hell.

Gannon hunkers down, takes a look. His whistle is almost appreciative. "I think you're right, Faraday. The experiment's over."

I don't like what I see in his eyes. It's probably the same look that's in mine.

Conroy's madly going through papers, knocking over test tube racks, scanning labels and print outs. I ask him if he's found a sample of strain-67 or Reaper, anything we can save before the whole place goes up. He keeps saying no.

"C'mon, c'mon," Gannon says at the door. "C'mon..."

"Francis..."

"Ahah!" There's the Eureka I was after. "Detectives! I may have found the solution."

The CSI pushes aside a stack of folders, beckons me to look at one. He's feverishly happy. "Your doctor, Chan was it?, he tried a lot of different combinations to find strain-67, left a lot on the cutting room floor, so to speak. I'm not surprised. No one's ever gone this far before. He's a very smart man."

"We don't have time for the inaugural meeting of the Dr Chan Fan Club," I say through gritted teeth. "What's your point?"

Conroy points to a computer print out. "My point is, while he was making strain-67, he was also looking for a way to cure it. To counteract the effects of the drug. And he found it. Look – here!"

He points to a row of numbers and letters that look like chemical equations. I'm reminded of earlier in the night when he showed my blood work to Gannon in the morgue. "I don't know what this shit means either, Francis."

"Saline," he says, clearly frustrated, "It means that a shot of saline will stop strain-67. It flushes the drug from your system. Neutralizes it. If you can inject saline into your brain, strain-67 won't have any effect. That is, if you do it fast enough."

Great. Yet another brain needle would make my afterlife complete. "How fast is fast enough?" I ask.

The pathologist shrugs. "Thirty seconds, maybe less."

"We ain't got thirty seconds now," Gannon says. The timer on the bomb ticks over to 4:32, 4:31. "We gotta go."

Conroy fills two needles from a drip bag of saline, passes them to me. His hands are shaking and it's time for him to leave. "Get what you can and get out of here,

Conroy," I say. "This is no place for the living."

The pathologist gives me a grateful smile as he shuffles papers into his arms. "You're all right, Faraday. Now that you're dead."

I take that as a compliment. Conroy leaves in a trail of paper as Gannon and I exit the lab. He'll get out in time but Gannon and I have four minutes, tops, to find Hob.

Gannon's already moving down the next corridor, shotgun raised, and I fall into step behind him. The burning red numbers of the timer stay in my thoughts. The small amount of time we have until Manhattan Psychiatric is blown to kingdom come gives me hope. Maybe the bad guys haven't left just yet. Hob said time goes slower when you're dead. Hopefully slow enough.

All the doors on this hallway are closed except for one. While Gannon checks the corner ahead, I peek through the open door and see an observation room, the wall taken up with a sheet of glass overlooking a white room. Same as the room they had me in. Only this room's got two dead men in it, not one.

Dr Xin Chan sits in a corner, head slumped against his chest. His lab coat, which had looked freshly starched when he stood over me with a needle full of Reaper, is now a mess of blood. Multiple gunshot wounds. One to the forehead, looks like two, maybe three to the chest. He'll relive with a splitting headache. That is, if they haven't already hit him with strain-67 and he wakes up before the C4 does. Even dead, the doctor's smiling. His teeth are smeared with blood.

The other dead man is familiar and it takes a moment before I realize who he is. Last time I saw him he was face down in an appetizer.

Stephen Trask looks much the same now (minus the bruschetta). Shocked. Pale. There's a black hole in his temple from where his dead wife's bullet turned him necro.

He bites at his fingernails, looking vaguely unsure how he, a man as rich and powerful as Donald Trump's corpse, could end up a prisoner in his own cell. Looks like Ole Hob did what he always does. Double cross. Never trust a dead gangster, I always say.

I contemplate just walking away, letting Trask and his mad scientist burn with the rest of their experiment, but something's niggling at me, something that isn't right. Something about Cherry and her escape from this place. Those damn questions never leave me alone.

A switch on the console says INTERCOM. I flick it.

Trask jumps when he hears the cackle of static, looks around like a trapped animal. "Who's there? God, please, who is it? Hello?"

"Why'd you do it, Trask?" I ask softly. "Why'd you dump Cheryl Hampton's body?"

He's spooked, wild eyed. His dead skin hangs in loose folds on his face and neck. Like me, he's had better days. "Who are you?" he asks crazily. "Who's there?"

"I thought she escaped," I say. "I thought, somehow, she'd found a way to get out of here. Maybe slipped past the doctor when he wasn't looking. Maybe used enough of the brainpower she had left after all the fucking drugs you pumped into her to figure a way out to the river. Hell, she could have dug her way out of her cell, for all I know. But she didn't. Did she?"

"I have money, lots of money and it's all yours," Trask pleads. "Help me, please!"

"See, Hob fucked up. He showed me what happened when strain-67 was given to one of his z-boys. The shit works fast. There's no way Cherry could have gotten out of here on her own after being injected. No way. Strain-67 works *too* damn fast."

"Th-th-there's a bomb! In the building! Help me! Please!"

"So that means you let her out. Or, more likely you had your mixed life twins take her and dump her somewhere where she'd be found, somewhere public. Somewhere across the river, so tracing her back to Manhattan Psychiatric would be impossible. Somewhere where word would spread fast that a dead girl isn't undead. Somewhere like Carl Schulz Park."

"PLEASE!" Trask is screaming, grayish-white spit hitting the glass as he pummels it with his fists. I like watching him squirm. How many times did Cherry hit the walls and no one came to save her?

"What were you going to do? Let New York tear itself apart and then have Omega step in like a savior with a ready-made weapon against the tide of the dead? Your stock's in the toilet, the company's going down. This is your way to stop a hostile takeover – this is the big project you've been working on. There's nothing that would stop a Newly Dead like strain-67. Nothing legal. In fact, I doubt the government would even sanction mass production of a drug like strain-67...not unless it was a national emergency. Like, say, a riot in a capital city?"

The Omega CEO is hammering the glass, turning his fists to bloody pulps. I'm still not going to unlock the door. I imagine Evelyn Trask, sitting in a jail cell somewhere, smiling. You should never guarantee satisfaction for your clients, but it's good when it happens.

"That's why you needed Grandpa Hob. That's why you let him burrow in deep. Omega was getting lab rats from the old corpse, necro kids that wouldn't be missed, but no – you needed more. You needed a war. Who better to give you one then a dead mobster? Well, it looks like he fucked you over, Trask. Looks like Hob's taken the war with him. And you're just another casualty."

Trask sinks to his knees, a blubbering mess. He's still begging to be let go but the words no longer make sense. They're not even words. Just sounds, whimpers.

That's not going to work on me either.

"I'm leaving you here, Trask. To die again."

The dead man jumps up and bashes the glass, hollering, crying, wailing. He's got less than three minutes of afterlife left.

I decide to twist the knife one more time. I click the intercom and say: "Go to Hell."

The door to the observation room must be soundproof. After it's closed behind me, I can't hear the screaming at all.

Chapter 24
The Big Kill

Gannon's outside, anxiously scanning the hallway.
"What'd you find?" he whispers.

"Nothing. Dead men."

"Yeah, well there's a couple of live ones around the corner I could use your help with. C'mon."

We slip up the hall, silent. The pump action feels light in my hands, like a toy, but I really want to shoot someone now, to let off some steam, and the shotgun's up for the job. Like me. Hob hasn't lost any points for double crossing Omega. His bullet tally's gone up again. *Two have paid, Cherry. Couple more to go.*

Around the bend are a pair of fuckers I was hoping we'd run into. I'd seen enough of their fists since the first time they'd knocked me out at The Closet Skeleton. The Arnie twins. One living, one dead, both assholes.

They're talking in front of a set of double doors that, according to the sign, lead to the loading dock, and I can just make out what the twins are saying.

"...conflict, dear brother. Conflict is what I feel."

"How so?"

"Were we not in the employ of the rotund gentleman? Yet, now we are in fact employees of the small gentleman. I am conflicted, is all."

"Ah, you think too much, brother o' mine. Let me

ask you – are we not, in fact, being paid more, now that we are, in fact, in the employ of the small gentleman?"

"This is true."

"Then what is the conflict?"

"Truly you are wise, my brother."

"As are you. Now, shall we? The party is set to start any minute. Methinks we should be elsewhere when it does."

Gannon must be able to sense my desire for mayhem, as he grips his own shotgun tight enough for his knuckles to go white. Either that or the bone's broken through his skin.

I count to three under my breath and as one we round the corner.

"FREEZE!" Gannon cries, all cop. "Hands up!"

The mixed life twins are pros and it only takes them a moment to react. Dutch, the dead one, bellows like a stuck pig and charges down the hallway towards us.

The living twin whirls off his Armani jacket and I finally understand how they did away with Cyrus Beaumont and Douglas Hampton III. Strapped to Butch's chest in a leather harness are dozens of beakers, their necks stuffed with rags. They look like Molotov cocktails but I'm guessing it's not vodka they're holding. Hydrochloric cocktail, anyone?

Butch lights a beaker and launches it. The missile explodes against the wall above my head, sending orange flame billowing to the ceiling. The skin on my face sizzles from the heat. That's gonna leave a mark.

Gannon fires, once, twice, and the shotgun makes gaping holes in Dutch's dead chest. But the Newly Dead hitman doesn't stop coming towards us like a freight train, leaping the fire that another one of his brother's acid bombs makes. He's a gorilla, even against the size of Gannon. And bullets ain't stopping him.

Inspiration hits me before he does. "Ray! Hold out

your shotgun!"

My ex-partner rolls away as a Molotov soars over his head, smashing into a fireball behind us. Gannon lands on the balls of his feet, looks at me dumbly.

"Just come here!" I yell.

He scuttles over and I grab the barrel of his Remington and shove mine into his hand. "If we hold them together, we just might be able to hold him back," I say.

"That's your plan?" Gannon's incredulous.

"You got a better one?"

Dutch rockets through the acidic smoke and slams into our makeshift dam break. The force of the necro hits me like a yellow cab doing 90mph. He reaches for my throat and even being dead doesn't hold back the fear of what he could do to me with those hands.

But Gannon's there, keeping it level, keeping us in the fight, and I'm glad he is, glad he's beside me for this. With an almighty grunt, Gannon slams the shotguns against the dead man's chest, rocking him back on his heels. It's enough for me to get my feet back and, as one, we push.

Dutch is backpedaling, arms pin wheeling, so I grab his jacket with one hand, heft the shotguns into his stomach and lift. Gotta keep him off balance or he'll be on us in a second.

His hands scrabble at the walls as we push, and acid fire sparks on his shoulders. He calls for Dutch like a lost child for mummy.

"Brother!" the living one yells. The Molotov he was about to light is forgotten in his hand. "What are you doing to my brother?"

"He's your brother!" I cry as he close the last few feet, fire licking at me from Dutch's smoldering corpse, turning the plastic stocks of the Remingtons to slag. "CATCH!"

Gannon and I heave and the dead Arnie crashes backwards into his brother. There's the sound of shattering glass as the Molotovs strapped to Butch's chest break against Dutch's back, then the pair are engulfed in an orange mushroom cloud of fire.

The flame rushes over me but the screams of the Arnies is a pleasant melody in my ears. There's a heaviness on my back, my jacket's on fire.

I roll away from the Arnie twins as they burn like an insane funeral pyre, dancing together as the hydrochloric strips the flesh from their bones, sizzles their skulls. They flop on the linoleum, a gaggle of body parts slowly melting away.

My jacket's turning to ash and I wrestle out of it, hit at the spots of fire on my forearms and thighs. It turns my fingers black. "Ray? You still with me?"

Gannon coughs beside me, stamping his feet to get rid of the fire at his pants cuffs. "Yeah," he splutters.

"You think the others heard us?"

"Yeah."

"We should go then."

"Yeah."

Gannon always did have a way with words. Butch and Dutch are twitching on the floor, the top halves of their bodies blackened. There's not much left. We step over them and go through the double doors. *One to go, Cherry. One more and then all the motherfuckers have paid.*

The doors lead to a storage room with a large, open roller door across from us. Starlight shines on a van being loaded up with metal cases. Past that is the river and past that is the pedestrian bridge that links Randall-Wards Island to Harlem. The fires look like they're still burning over there. Then I remember the fire that's coming to Manhattan Psychiatric, and I focus on what's in front of me.

A half a dozen z-boys, recognizable by their lack of

fashion sense, are packing boxes into the back of the van. Grandpa Hob bustles around from the front of the van, checking his watch incessantly and waving his walking cane at the necros to get them moving. Probably two minutes, maybe one and a half left before the building blows. No wonder the sonofabitch looks worried.

"That van can't leave here," I say.

Gannon nods grimly. "I'll get the van. You get Hob."

He slips into the darkness made by a stack of old crates. He's gone left, so I go right. As loudly as possible.

"HOB!" I call. "You weren't going to leave without saying goodbye, were you?"

The z-boys look up in alarm, and Grandpa Hob spins around. His face is priceless. "How...?"

"Guess you can't keep a good man down," I say, stepping out into the light. "Or a dead one."

"I obviously put too much stock in Omega's twins. You should never trust men who jump ship, hmm, Mr Faraday. A mistake I won't be making again." He signals to his z-boys. "Get that fool."

The toughs snarl as they come towards me. All of them are young, the eldest around twenty when he died. They look tough, probably bangers taken down in a drive-by or another gang, a mixed bunch of Dead Americans who ain't scared of nothing, just ask them, they'll tell you. They look like they're about to do more than just tell me, though. Where the fuck is Gannon?

As if on cue, the back tires of the van scream against the tarmac as Gannon hits the gas. A few boxes tumble out, smashing on the ground, and Hob gapes like a dead goldfish. Score one for the good guys.

The z-boys stop, look to their grandpa for help. "Don't just stand there!" the old necro howls. "Get the van! Get the van, idiots!"

They forget me and throw themselves after the

speeding van, a couple getting handholds on the doors and sides. Gannon grinds the gears – he was never good with stick shift – and the van lurches out the door and into the moonlight.

I take the opportunity and make for Hob but the old corpse is quicker than he looks. He spits a curse and runs, heading out the roller door. What was the bullet tally again? Shit, it doesn't matter. I'll just empty my gun into him.

I'm hot on his dead heels when, from the corner of my eye, I catch sight of something swinging at me. Desperately I duck and roll as something hard and metal raises sparks from the floor.

I come up face-to-face with Charlie.

"Fuck."

The z-boy is a patchwork man, his chest and arms riddles with stitches. Hob must have put all his pieces back together. That's another bullet.

Charlie's got the same machete he used to cut off Dorothy's head, and he takes another swipe at me that keeps me on my back.

"Not so tough without your train, huh, heroman," Charlie growls, cutting at the ground where my head had been an instant earlier. "You gonna pay for what you did to me."

The machete bites into my shoulder. I hear bone crunch and suddenly my arm's dead weight, swinging at my side. Charlie slashes down again and again, and I can barely keep away from the wicked knife edge.

Gannon's gunning the engine, taking the van in a wide arc as if he means to come back and get me. The van's covered with z-boys, crawling with the stinking neccers. One's on the roof, inching towards the windscreen.

I kick out and hit Charlie's groin with a satisfying crunch, making him stumble backwards.

I roll onto my feet and the shotgun's too far away.
I draw my Beretta.

His grin is evil. I didn't think a kick in the balls
would keep him down. I suspected he wouldn't have any.

"Whatcha gonna do with that, heroman? You can't
kill me."

"You're right. You can't kill a dead man. All you
can do is slow him down."

I aim for his kneecap and shoot. The bone in his
leg explodes in a gush of black blood, the leg severing at the
knee and dropping Charlie to the ground. The machete
spins away but he's still got one leg. I take that out, too,
and the gunshot echoes in the loading bay.

He grunts and grabs for me, snagging my shirt.
The move pulls him completely away from his cut off legs
and they flop on the ground like dying fish. If I had the
time, I'd throw up.

Charlie's clinging to my chest. With only one arm
working I'm no match for him, legs or not. I need to get
him off me.

He bites at my face like a rabid animal, tearing a
strip of flesh from my cheek. He's going to bite through
my skull to get to my brain. Figures. The only zombie in
the world who wants to eat brains and he has to be the one
I fight.

Gannon's gunning the van back towards the ramp
of the loading bay. The z-boys swarm over the vehicle,
one at the door reaching in, another slamming its head
against the windscreen trying to shatter the glass and get
inside. Gannon's face is frantic behind the spider web of
cracks. I've never seen him look so determined. He's
coming and he's coming fast.

Charlie's grip is like steel, can't shake him. My
Beretta's against his kidneys and I fire once, twice, but he
doesn't stop, doesn't let go. I may as well be pillow
fighting.

"I'm gonna fuck you up!" the z-boy hisses in my face.

The van hits the ramp, the chassis grinding against metal and throwing sparks. The engine roars as the tires leave the ground. Death is coming and it drives stick.

Surprisingly I don't want to die. Not for good, not now. With an effort that leaves black spots dancing before my eyes, I wrench up my gun, put it to Charlie's chin, and pull the trigger.

The bullet goes into his head and shatters the top of his skull. Grey chunks fly and his grip on my shoulders loosens enough for me to muscle him free.

In the instant he hits the ground, the van looms as large as God and I throw myself for the open air. The van flies over the top of me, close enough that the bumper bar swishes my hair, and I hit the ramp and roll.

Charlie doesn't get off so good. When the van touches ground, the front tire smashes into his face. The cracking of his skull is the sweetest music I've ever heard.

There must only be seconds left before the bomb goes and Gannon isn't stopping. The van plows through the storage room, sending z-boys flying, crashing through boxes and crates.

Gannon hits the park brake and the van turns on its side and slams into the double doors leading into the old hospital. The vehicle rocks on its shocks and the damage must have opened the fuel line, as fire licks to life beneath the tires.

I see Gannon through the broken windscreen. "GO!" he screams. "GET THE FUCK OUT OF HERE, FARADAY!"

But I don't. There are so many things I want to tell him. Not the least of which that he isn't as big an asshole as I make out.

Then the fire flares and the van explodes, taking my ex-partner with it.

Ray...

I...

I run for the river, cradling my busted arm, whimpering but choking it back. Outside the door is Charlie's machete and I scoop the long knife up. May come in handy.

Up ahead Ole Hob's spindly shadow is making for the pedestrian bridge. If he thinks he's going home to Harlem, he's got another thing coming.

I run and run and run and just when I think the bomb might be a dud, Manhattan Psychiatric erupts like a volcano.

The force of the explosion knocks me on my ass and the rush of heat is worse then the Arnie twins' acid Molotovs. The ground is suddenly lit up like daylight as twenty-odd floors of hospital is consumed by flame. You can see the fire from Rhode Island. What the mental patients failed to do a year ago, tonight is complete. Hob's little fire sale is a success.

But not completely. I'm coming, Hob. And I'm bringing hell with me.

Chapter 25
My Gun Is Quick

By the time I've reached the steps, the old neccer is already on the bridge. Grandpa Hob's walking cane tap-tap-taps the bridge like a coward's heartbeat as he hobbles along. Looks like he's running out of steam.

I scale the steps, dragging Charlie's machete after me and glad the z-boy didn't cut one of my legs off or Hob would be harder to chase. The river's a smudge of dark beneath the bridge and I picture Cherry floating like a dead angel in the shadowy water. Monsters like Ole Hob deserve to die like that. Not you, Cherry.

"HOB!" I yell. "You can't run forever!"

He doesn't intend to. The old necro reaches into his coat and draws what looks like a toy gun, all plastic and see through. What the hell is he doing with that?

"I don't need to outrun you, Mr Faraday. Not when I have this!"

He shoots and there's a whooshing sound, and a barbed dart appears in my temple with a meaty thud. For a moment I don't know what's going on. Stupid fucker brought a tranquilizer dart to a gunfight.

Then my head seems to go cold. The machete drops.

I fall to my knees, legs suddenly not working anymore.

Fuck.

The fucker's hit me with strain-67.

Grandpa Hob's laughter is chilling. "You like it, Mr Faraday, hmm? Hasn't quite got the same kick as my Reaper, but Dr Chan told me a certain buzz goes along with it. He told me before I killed him, of course. Just like I'm killing you now."

I curl into a ball. The drug works fast, I've seen it on Linus, and already my limbs are shaking. The iciness in my heart spreads to my arms. Cold, so cold.

My hands twitch as I reach into my pocket.

Hob's close to me now. Smug, confident, speaking right in my ear. "You just couldn't stay away, could you? That's the problem, nowadays. Back when, you put a bullet in a fool or throw him in the river and that was that. He didn't come back. Now – hell, you never know if you get your enemies good enough that they won't come knocking on your door again."

Strain-67 is pounding in my head like a drum beat. My knees buckle, sprawling me on my stomach, and I can't move anything below my chest. I figure there's about twenty seconds before I'm done for good.

Numbed fingers close over the saline needles Conroy gave me. If I can keep my hands working, I'll live.

Hob taps the tranquilizer gun against my head. "But that's what's so good about strain-67, Mr Faraday. Just like the good old days. You hit 'em once and they stay down for good. Now anything's possible."

I groan, hunch over. The saline needle shakes in my hand. One good shot, all I need is one good shot without Hob seeing me. Need to get the needle in my brain. That's what Conroy said.

There's a rushing in my ears that's not the Hudson River.

Hob turns wistful. "I'd love to stay and watch you die *again*, Mr Faraday, but I have work to do. Since you've blown up all my lovely drugs, I shall have to find a chemist who can make me more."

The old neccer waves something in front of my face. A black box. A hard drive. "Of course, with Dr Chan's notes, that shouldn't prove too difficult."

Is this what death, real death, is like? Confusion, darkness, numbness. Regret, fear. A nagging sense that something been's left unfinished, something vitally important.

Hob laughs. "Goodbye, Mr Faraday. We shall not be seeing each other again."

Grey mucus drips from my nose. Is it my brain turning to mush? Probably. My right arm won't do what it's told and my left looks like a drunk with the DTs. I figure my nose is my best shot. No pun intended.

I grip the needle and stab upwards.

My body convulses. Warm, salty liquid gushes from my mouth, my nose, even leaks from my eyes. A great warmth spreads through my body, like stepping from shadow into the noon day sun. It's a feeling I thought I'd never experience again, now that I'm dead. I feel alive. The saline courses through my system, flushing the strain-67 from my brain. Like a heaviness is lifted from my shoulders.

In a moment the coldness in my head is gone and I thank God for making Francis Conroy such a nerd. Dammit. How many times has Conroy saved my life now? Yet another thing to thank Hob for. I hate that type of debt.

The old zombie's walking away slowly, twirling his walking stick as if he's enjoying the view, cradling the hard drive in the crook of his arm like a lover's hand.

He doesn't look back as I stand up shakily, dropping the spent saline needle. He thinks he's won. The fires in Harlem burn my eyes. Hob is a shadow. But all I can see is Cherry.

In five steps I'm at his back, machete raised.

He hears me coming and turns. To see the fear in his dead, white eyes is enough to make my year.

I think about every goddamn step of this case, everything I've had to go through since Cherry Hampton turned up dead, everyone who's suffered, every life that's been fucked, every afterlife that's been cut short. Every fucking thing that's happened because of this fucking bag of bones that calls itself Grandpa Hob.

And there's really only one thing left to do.

I swing and the machete bites into his neck with a satisfying thunk.

Hob drops his cane and the hard drive, more shocked at seeing me alive than anything else. Bony fingers claw at my chest as I jam my knee into his stomach, pinning him to the railing. I have strength I didn't know was possible.

"But I gave you strain-67...how...?" he splutters.

"Anything's possible, Hob, remember? Welcome to the good old days."

The second cut to his neck must sever something, because his head flops onto his shoulder. By the third cut the machete's biting into spinal cord and I have to saw. The old neccer cries out as his skin falls away like mummified bandages, yellow-grey with age like rotten paper. With one last swing, I lop off his head and send it tumbling across the bridge.

Hob's body slumps against the railing and the arms flail at me. The body's lost without the head, like a twitching tail without a lizard. I grab its ankles and hoist, and after a few seconds there's a splash when the corpse hits the water.

The neccer's head is lying on its cheek. I pick it up by the severed end of the spinal cord, holding him upside down. I want to see how he feels being on the other end of the stick.

Hob laughs in my face.

"What are you going to do now, Mr Faraday? The only strain-67 left in the world was in my pocket and you just threw into the river. You can't kill me. Are you going to take me in, then? How many times have you tried to arrest me?"

I stoop to pick up the hard drive. This little black box holds death. For all. I hurl it into the river.

"Fourteen arrests," I say. "Fifteen if you count this one."

Hob grins. Being upside down, it's more of a frown. "With your ex-wife as my lawyer, nothing you say will stick. I'll be free before the first news report goes to air. I'll find another body soon enough, plenty of dead parts for sale in this town."

"Tell me about Cherry," I say.

"Who?"

"The girl, Hob. The one you dumped in the river."

Brown liquid is seeping from Hob's mouth. He's so old there's no blood left. Only rotten formaldehyde and rancid snot. "That little neccer slut? She was nobody. Just another child of the city hooked on smack and dead cock. They're a dime a dozen in America, Mr Faraday, you of all people should know that."

My knuckles whiten. "What do you mean?"

The old neccer chuckles, the sound bubbly from the shit pouring out of his mouth. "Nothing happens in this city without my say-so. Who do you think Gray Gary J got the gear from to make his little harem of dead hookers? Everything is mine. Every soul, every street, every afterlife. Mine. I am New York. I own it.

"I even own you, Mr Faraday."

That bar in Tribeca crowds my thoughts. A shit-eating grin and a pair of dead blue eyes. But the thoughts are getting easier to push away. When I think about Cherry.

It was all you, wasn't it Hob?

"What are you going to do?" he asks. "You can't kill me and you can't stop me, Mr Faraday."

I bring his face close to mine. Smile. "You know what, Hob? You're right. I can't kill you and I can't stop you. But I can do this."

I pitch Ole Hob's head over the side.

He hollers all the way down.

I scream after him, "LET'S SEE YOU FIND A BODY IN HELL, YOU CRUSTY OLD FUCK!"

There's a splash as the head hits the water and Grandpa Hob is gone.

I imagine his severed head falling beneath the surface, falling like concrete shoes, the black water swallowing him the same way it did to Cherry. The neccer won't feel the cold but he'll be able to see the nothingness, hear the silence, know that all that waits for him is the bottom, the pit, the lowest circle of a hell reserved just for crusty old demons like him.

Or maybe a shark will get him. That would be good, too.

Long after the noise of the splash has died away, I lean against the railing of the bridge, smoking a Death and looking at the lights of my city, at the fires burning in Harlem, at the inferno at my back that was once Manhattan Psychiatric.

And I think about Cherry and all the shit that came along with her. And for once I don't think it's too bad a night to be alive or dead.

EP ¡ ¡ogue

Two days later and I'm starting to smell. Thankfully I can't tell myself, but judging by the looks I'm getting from the living people at *Lou's*, my decomposition is a social faux pas akin to letting your German Shepherd shit on a fire hydrant and not bagging it. Somehow the other people's discomfort makes me comfortable.

On the other side of the booth, Alison Kastle is sipping a Coke and digesting everything I just told her. Kastle with a K had wanted a story. I gave her one, told her everything, starting from when I saw Cheryl Hampton's deader than dead body floating off Carl Schulz Park. Cherry, Hob, Omega – everything from the Closet Skeleton to Manhattan Psychiatric. I left out the bits where I was beaten up, though. Artistic license.

When I finish, Kastle touches the red scarf knotted over the stitches of her slashed throat. By her frown, she doesn't believe me.

"I don't know, Jonny. I don't think I can run with this. The cops say the hospital on Randall-Ward's was blown up by lifers. The bodies they found belonged to homeless dead, most of them teenage runaways who were known to hang out at the old hospital. There hasn't been a whiff of Omega's involvement in any of it – the only news from Omega is that Stephen Trask's gone into hiding after stepping down as CEO, which made the stocks go up ten points. No one's been charged yet with the murders of Cyrus Beaumont and Douglas Hampton because the police figure they were part of the lifist riots. Grandpa Hob's lying low and Cheryl Hampton is still officially a suicide."

Kastle shrugs. "I just don't know, Jonny."

She needs proof and I'm glad I stopped in to see Conroy on my way to *Lou's*.

Conroy had been wearing one of his Hawaiian shirts, heading out to pick up Dorothy the head on his way to the park. Apparently Kastle gave him her number and they'd hit it off over the phone. First date was today. Don't ask me how you date a head. You can't really go on long walks, can you?

Luckily I caught him before he left, and he gave me two things. One is a folder of papers he took from Manhattan Psychiatric before it blew. A folder I'm now sliding across the table to Kastle.

She flicks through it eagerly. "What is it?"

"What you need. Proof. Lab results, admittance records, shopping lists and library cards for Omega's little experiment. Names, dates, email accounts. You should have more than enough to kick over a few rocks."

Kastle closes the folder, smoothes her hand over the front lovingly. "Yes...yes indeed. This I can use." She gives me a Cheshire grin. "Wow. Jon Faraday comes to me with answers instead of questions. Being dead suits you, Jonny. You're a changed man."

I bolt my bourbon. "Don't start rumors."

"All I know is you were never this forthcoming when you were a cop. Ray was always the one who talked the most out of the two of you..." She trails off, face stricken.

Women. I think they bring shit up just to dance around it.

"I heard what happened," she says. "He died in the line of duty...didn't he?"

I've been thinking about Gannon a lot these last couple of days. Remembering. He was always the better cop. Always the one most likely to do what was right, while I was just along for the ride. Detective Ray Gannon.

My partner. The TV says he died trying to save Newly Dead children from Manhattan Psychiatric, only he didn't get out in time. I know he gave his afterlife up to do what was right, just like he'd always wanted.

"Yeah," I say. I don't want her to know the details. It's enough that Ray will get a funeral with honors. If she knew about me being with him at the old hospital, questions would be asked and the answers would have to come from me. My name is mud at Police Plaza and I don't want to drag Gannon down here with me. Ray Gannon, hero, is a good story to stick to.

Kastle sidles out of the booth, folder in hand. She has a burning in her eyes that tells me she's going to get to the bottom of it. Or the top, considering how many Omega letterheads she has in her hot hand. Journalists *are* good for something.

"Well...thanks, Jonny. I mean it."

I tip her my glass. "Welcome."

She bites her lip. "Give me a call sometime. You know the number." Kastle turns to go and adds over her shoulder: "You still look good – even for a dead guy."

Kastle with a K could never let me have the last word. She sashays out of the bar, mobile phone cupped to her dead ear. She's on the case. I'll see the fruits of her labors tonight at 6.

I order another bourbon. I'm halfway done by the time Brenda Barrett shows up. Ten minutes early, as always. My ex-wife swishes into the booth, tight in a skirt suit. She orders a Manhattan. She doesn't look like a woman in mourning but at least her suit's black.

Brenda doesn't say anything, just stares at me while she waits on the waitress. It's going to be one of those conversations again.

After her drink arrives and she hasn't touched it, I surprise myself by saying, "I...I'm sorry about Ray."

I wanted to talk about why I asked her here, but

Gannon slipped out first.

"I really am sorry. I...I may never forgive you and him for sleeping together after I was kicked off the force. But I never wanted Gannon to die. I'm not that big of an asshole."

Brenda nods. She's trying hard to keep it inside. "I know you're not. I...I'm sorry about Ray, too. The last thing I said to him...I don't want to think about it."

Ray had said she'd left him because he was dead. I can guess what their last conversation had been.

Brenda coughs, and then says, "But we're not here to talk about Ray. Are we?"

"No," I say.

I reach into my jacket and pull out something I photocopied before leaving Conroy's office earlier. A piece of paper the Kastle doesn't have.

"Do you know what this is?" Brenda shakes her head. "I call it leverage."

I flick the paper to her and she reads it quickly. Her brow furrows. "Where did you get this?"

"Not important. What's important is the name mentioned in the last paragraph. Recognize it?"

She doesn't answer. Of course she recognizes the name. She'd know it anywhere. It's the same name on all those checks she gets.

"Grandpa Hob," I say. "What you've got there is proof that your best client, and a man generally regarded to be the necro drug king of New York City, is directly involved with the production and illegal testing of pharmaceutical narcotics and the incarceration and torture of dozens of Newly Dead children. The press will have a field day. I should know, I've already talked to them."

Brenda gasps. "You went public with this?"

I smile grimly. "Not all of it. Not this particular memo, one I'm sure the DA's office would give their right arm to get a hold of. When I read this I thought Hob must be slipping in his old age, letting his name show up on a memo from Stephen Trask confirming the date and time *Hob's shipment* would arrive at Manhattan Psychiatric. Then I realised the memo was internal; Ole Hob wouldn't have known about it. Then I thought how someone looking in the right place and asking the right questions could link Hob to Omega. And with what I've given Kastle, plus this particular piece of paper, that would be more than enough to indict the old dead fart. Do you see what I'm getting at?"

She does. I can tell by the set of her jaw. "What do you want?"

I've got her. "Like I said, leverage. I'm not naïve enough to believe Hob's gone for good. Sure, it's gonna take him a while to chew his way across the bottom of the Hudson River. But I know him. He'd do it just to spite me. And I figure, once he does, he's going to come looking for the man who put him there.

"This," I point to the memo, "will only see the light of day if Hob does me in for good. I want you to tell him that, Brenda. This is my get-out-jail-free card. Tell Ole Hob to forgive and forget. Otherwise he'll be the one going down for good."

Like a true lawyer she's inscrutable. I wonder how her *selective reality* is feeling today. Reality isn't subjective, Brenda. It's all around you. Whether you like it or not.

"Fine," she begrudges. "I'll pass your message onto my client. Should my client reappear, that is." Clipped fingernails fold the photocopy and put it in her coat pocket as she stands. Meeting adjourned.

But I can't let her go without saying, "You always said you never knew anything about Hob's criminal affairs. Now you do, Brenda. You should get yourself a new client."

For the first time in a long time, Brenda Barrett cracks. There's the tinniest edge of fragility to her voice when she says, "I would, Jon. But sometimes you can get in so deep, there's no way out. Not if you want to protect the people you love."

She leaves me with an untouched Manhattan and the bill. In deep? That's what happens when you sell your soul to a devil like Grandpa Hob, Brenda. There's no backing out on the debt.

Lou's is getting claustrophobic – the afternoon crowd is filled with Dead American dock workers coming off 20-hour shifts and looking for the warm dulling of thought that comes with too much beer – so I hit the streets.

My Chevy, newly rescued from the police impound yard after serving two to three days on a parking rap, thrums up Broadway. They put out the last fires in Harlem yesterday but you can still see the smoke.

New York's like that. She's got a short memory and she's not the type to dwell. New York moves on, and as I roll past streets in which the living and the dead are walking and working and lying and loving, I wonder if Ole Hob was right in what he said. That life is cheap in a dead world. Too cheap. Maybe he's right.

But, being dead, I've had time to think about it. And I think, living or dead, we're all Americans. And that should count for something at least.

I'm heading for the Brooklyn Bridge and the address Conroy gave me along with the files. His scrawl of handwriting leads me to a bargain embalmer in an office above a bowling alley in Queens.

The dead receptionist is ruddily perfect, as if she was just nipped and sucked this morning. I wait between a flabby Dead Asian reading a five year old *Time* magazine and a dead woman whose stomach is so bloated with gas she keeps farting with great embarrassment. Thankfully the mention of cousin Conroy lets me skip the line and soon enough I get in to see the doctor.

Then again, doctor is such a strong word. Conroy's cousin – who turns out to be a beefy version of Conroy sans the moustache – tells me to sit on a metal table as he arrays his tools, scalpels, saws and these strange things that look like guns hooked up by tubes to silver canisters marked with the word FORMALIN.

I ask him how long he's been doing this, and he must notice my unease.

"Relax," the embalmer says. "You won't feel a thing. Now – take off your clothes and lie on your stomach."

As he turns dials on the canisters and checks the pressure, I strip and get on the table. The metal's probably cold but I can't feel it. It's taking some getting used to, this numbness. But I don't mind. When you're getting embalmed, anything will do to take your mind off it.

Conroy's cousin chats about what he's going to do – flushing out organs, adding formaldehyde, that sort of thing – and I tune out. I don't know why he's telling me. I don't really want to know the intimate details. He's definitely related to Conroy.

"Now," the embalmer says , "I just have to put the formalin pump in your rectum."

Thinking of Conroy makes me wonder how his date with the severed head was going. No offence but I think Dorothy could do better. Conroy can sometimes be a real pain in the a-

Hang on – where's the pump going?

THE END

ABOUT THE AUTHOR

Luke Keioskie has been a professional writer since the millennium turned and the world didn't end. A one time lecturer in Creative Writing, he's currently a web editor by day and a novelist by night. He has a Doctor of Creative Arts and spends far too much time at the beach.

www.severedpress.com